(IR)RATIONAL

FEARS

William Sterling

ASIN: B0B57P6KCL

ISBN: 9798839879553

Imprint: Independently published

For Craig, Sabrina, and all the Monsters that might be in their Closets

My books contain various scenes which could potentially trigger a negative response in readers. If you have any topics which are off limits to you and would like to check for "trigger warnings" before reading IRRATIONAL FEARS, a list of topics breached in each of my books can be found by following the QR code below.

I hope this helps create a safe and comfortable reading experience for you all.

If you would rather avoid any sort of spoilers, feel free to disregard the QR code and turn the page.

TABLE OF CONTENTS

Flowers For Deborah

Deborah's funeral was held on June 21st. The day was overcast and that was probably for the best. Nobody liked to attend funerals in the rain, but so long as the clouds didn't get everybody all wet, then their presence would be good. They would lend an appropriately grey and dreary atmosphere to the afternoon's agenda, making it feel like the whole universe was in mourning along with Matt and the rest of the neighborhood.

At Matt's request, everybody had brought little plastic flowers to decorate Deborah's coffin. They had obliged and now a rainbow of red, purple, and blue petals carpeted her final resting place.

Deborah had always complained about Matt bringing home real flowers. Whether it was for her birthday, their anniversaries, or any other occasion, Deborah always said that real flowers made her sad because she hated thinking of something so beautiful being plucked and left to die on her behalf. She even refused a bouquet for her wedding.

Plastic flowers seemed like the perfect alternative, though.

Plastic flowers didn't have to be uprooted or sacrificed on anybody's behalf. Plastic flowers were created to be pretty, to be eternal, and to never wither or die.

Deborah would have loved them.

Matt shuffled his feet and looked at the ground as Father Thomas stepped forward.

He began the funeral the way that he always did; by thanking everybody for coming, by saying a few nice words about Deborah, and by talking about what a light Deborah had been for the rest of the community.

The pastor told a short, funny story about when, two years ago, Deborah had accidentally made cookies for the neighborhood potluck using baking soda instead of sugar. Deborah had never been known as much of a cook, but with her, it had always been the thought that counted. Whether her cookies were made with baking soda or sugar, they had always been made with love. And Deborah had never shown up to the potluck without love.

Everybody laughed at the memory of the awful cookies and the sounds of their catharsis were just loud enough to drown out the noises from inside the coffin.

At the front of the cul-de-sac, the Sheriff's Station and the Fire Department had parked vehicles in a formation to block the main road. It was said that their presence was meant to give the mourners some privacy, although that reasoning had always fallen flat with Matt. Who was going to be out and about right now, driving through neighborhoods, interrupting funerals? It didn't make sense.

But despite the questionable nature of their presence, the officers and the firemen had maintained a respectful distance from the neighborhood's proceedings, so everybody had learned to silently accept and tolerate their audience.

Still, Matt found himself distractedly gazing at the blue and red flashing lights, zoning out through the middle of Father Thomas' monologue.

It was shameful. Matt should have been focused on the moment. That was his wife in the coffin after all, covered by a blanket of pretty plastic flowers.

Matt refocused as Father Thomas dove into the more serious portion of the ceremony.

Father Thomas' voice dropped to almost a whisper when he spoke of the old gods and their hunger. He spoke of the pain that the world had suffered in the middle of the century, and he spoke of the rituals which the neighborhoods had developed, years ago, to satiate the devils' desires.

The neighbors all nodded their heads in collective understanding as Father Thomas produced the box of flint and steel which had been passed to him by the priesthood. The Father lit his own torch first, willfully ignoring the muffled screams that had grown louder throughout the ceremony.

Father Thomas' torch was used to light Mr. Goodman's, which was used to light Mrs. Bachman's, and so on, all the way around the circle until Matt lit his own torch on the flame from Mr. Hampton's torch.

It was Matt's right, and his duty, as Deborah's husband, to be the one who ignited the pyre.

He hesitated, the way that Matt had seen other loved ones hesitate time and time again. He had never really understood this moment when he was just an observer. But now that it was his turn, Matt struggled against a last second flood of self-doubt and remorse.

He closed his eyes and steeled himself for what had to be done. He remembered what it had been like when the demon Flereous last ravaged the Earth. To this day you could still see the shadows of his first victims scorched into the concrete in Kansas City.

So many people had died that day.

Never again.

This ritual needed to be done.

Opening his eyes, Matt saw the smoke from other neighborhoods' fires already rising into the air.

With a long breath and a single tear, Matt touched his torch to the woodpile.

Deborah's pounding and shrieking inside the coffin increased to a desperate crescendo as the kindling caught and the first flames engulfed the old, gas-cured wooden planks of the coffin.

The thing went up like a matchbox as Matt joined hands with the other people from the cul-de-sac, and they sang the old hymns, watching as the smoke rose, the heated air shimmered, and the plastic flowers on the coffin curled.

STORY NOTES

My first baby!

I wrote this short story originally for the Write Hive short story collection. The theme was to write something with the line "and the plastic curled" worked in. From there I was able to take my hatred of using real flowers for ceremonies, my preference for plastic flowers because they're reusable, and then just reverse engineer some reason that they would be melting and curling away.

The story ended up being very Wicker Man meets Channel Zero's No Way House, huh? Taking the quaint little suburban neighborhood where nothing bad ever happens and making it the epicenter for something dreadful. I think there's a full novel to be made from this idea. There are lots of elements to this world that could be fun to explore and if this ends up being the opening chapter to some bigger project, don't be surprised. But in the meantime I'll forever be proud of my second-place winning, quick, punchy little baby.

The Lake House

2009 was turning out to be the worst drought in Marie's lifetime. Sure, 2000 had been bad, but it hadn't managed to burn away the lakes, kill the crops, or decimate the wildlife the way 2009 was doing.

Marie scowled, arms crossed across her chest as she looked out across the red clay wasteland that ran up against her back yard. Her rowboat sat beached, still tethered to its dock but so far away from water that the boat looked comically lost. Dead algae browned and withered all along the dry, cracked red clay beach, scorched to death by the Georgian sun. The song "Summertime Sadness" made loops in Marie's head.

Maybe Lana Del Rey wrote the song for lakes like this.

Either the worst storm in centuries was gonna have to fill the lake back up, or Marie's "lake front property" was going to be dramatically mislabeled for a while. More than that, she was heartsick for the water grasses, trees, and lily pads that were suddenly abandoned, baking in the sun. She was fairly certain the lily pads belonged to a lotus plant that would bloom the following spring. On her way back, she would scoop it to join the jungle growing on her screen porch.

Marie tightened her sandals, pulled her hair up into a ponytail, and began walking towards where the shoreline had retreated. She could see the red-brown outline of the house from here. Not her house. The one she'd bought was behind her, situated safely on what was *supposed* to be dry land. No, Marie was walking towards the newly discovered lake house. The one which had begun to rise, back in May, from the depths of Lake Lanier, as the drought pulled the water line back farther and farther.

A local had to explain the history of the lake to Marie; told her all about Oscarville. Oscarville was the town they had flooded to make the lake oh, maybe a hundred years ago?

Nobody else cared about the submerged town anymore. For the people that had always lived here, the fact that a town sat down there in the depths was just another thing they'd grown accustomed to. Like football on the weekends and gun nuts on their ballots, the people in Forsyth County just knew that's the way things were. Didn't feel any sort of an itch to poke around the houses that rose up from the lake whenever a drought hit. But for Marie, Nashville didn't have anything like this. When she saw that chimney floating past her back yard for the first time, she'd freaked right the fuck out. She'd watched it as the weeks went by, growing taller and taller above the surface until finally the roof peeked out along with it. Then the tops of walls. Then, finally, today, a door frame.

The whole door hadn't emerged yet. Just a few inches worth of the top of the frame. But it was enough to show Marie where the entrance was, and there was enough of a gap between it and the roof that Marie knew air must be getting into the house. She could go in there now without worry about drowning or suffocating in the darkness.

She approached the mud-caked structure with a nervous sort of excitement. She didn't expect to find anything in the house. It was just going to be fun to go exploring. Pretending she was an archaeologist or something crazy like that, poking around the ruins of a lost civilization. And, as far fetched as that sounded, it wasn't too terribly far from the truth.

Oscarville had been flooded in 1912 after a long, dark history pocketed by racial violence, gentrification, you name it. Everything the Civil Rights Movement had worked to fix. And heaven knew that shit was still going on in the modern day, but still. The house, the town, felt like a time capsule of sorts. A muddy, rotting, algae infested time capsule. Rumor had it that when the town was flooded, people were evacuated so quickly they hadn't had time to pack. They just got rushed out before the wheels of progress...or she guessed the waves of progress more appropriately... nipped at their heels.

Maybe she would find a dead body.

The morbid thought invaded Marie's thoughts and gave her pause as her toes found the water. She had her bathing suit on and a snorkel in her right hand.

Did she really want to go searching through the house? What if she found something gross. Like, sure, a dead body. Would she want to keep living in her own house, knowing something like that was in her back yard?

She shifted her weight back and forth, looked around. Nobody else was here. She could sort of see Mr. Selby's house through the trees to her right, but the seclusion of this inlet was what had really drawn her to move here. Nobody would disturb her as she explored.

And yeah. You know what? Screw it. She was going exploring.

Marie patted the Ziploc bag that contained her phone, made sure it was still pinned snugly between her bathing suit and her hip, then splashed into the water, wading in until she was floating, treading water lightly, her toes poking at the goop along the lake floor before she lost her resolve. She swam towards the doorway with clumsy, but effective strokes. Marie had never been the strongest swimmer. In her mind the lake was better for floating around in a boat, getting a suntan, drinking some margs instead of actually, you know, swimming in. But today called for exceptions to be made.

She splashed up to the house and grabbed the bottom of the roof-line for support. It was just a couple feet over the water and with her arm outstretched, she grasped it easily.

The layer of mud and algae which coated the walls of the house were incredible, the associated smell grotesque. The aroma of long dead, decayed fish washed over her and made her nauseous, again testing her resolve. If this was how bad it smelled on the outside, what would it be like inside the house?

She reached forward and poked at the mud above the door frame, wanting to test its depth and a layer of sludge at least five inches deep scraped away with her effort.

Gross.

Cool.

She leaned forward and grasped the top of the door frame, then took a deep breath and plunged underwater, pulling herself down, around, and through the threshold, popping back up on the other side into an air pocket of total darkness.

It was so crazy.

Below her the water glowed with a strange green tint as light from the outside world illuminated the lake. But here inside the house, none of that light broke through. The roof was still intact somehow. Any cracks in the walls or the shingles overhead had been shored up by the algae, leaving behind a perfect pocket of darkness.

Marie pulled the Ziploc bag from her bathing suit and fumbled with her phone through the plastic until she got the flashlight turned on.

Turning the light on was a mistake. She would know that later. Everything that ever had been or ever would be in that house was drawn to the light. When a place has rested for so long in perfect darkness, such a sudden introduction of light was a threat. A danger to be exterminated. Evil never takes kindly to being exposed.

But, as she often was, Marie was unaware.

No, all Marie knew when her flashlight first came on were the words in the house. Words and symbols covered the walls, defying rational

IRRATIONAL FEARS

explanation. With every other surface in the house smothered by detritus and dirt, how were these walls clear enough to host words?

THE NIGHT RIDERS AREN'T THROUGH WITH YOU.

Well that seemed ominous....

FIENDS OF HELL HAVE NO PLACE HERE.

The Night Riders and the Fiends of Hell? Were those biker gangs? Stupid club names for some kids that had snuck in here before her? Yeah. Sure. Maybe some dumb kids had already come out here, at night while Marie was sleeping. Maybe they'd cleared the mud from the walls and painted up their graffiti, tagging the location that they figured they and only they would ever see. It was dangerous to do that. There were so many stories about this Lake being cursed. People having accidents that could barely be explained. Kids going underwater and never resurfacing. Marie just hoped any pranksters that snuck onto her property were careful about their adventures, like she was being.

Curiosity unabated, Marie turned to scan the rest of the walls with her light.

A stack of bricks against the wall showed where the chimney was located. More graffiti told something of OSCAR'S REVENGE.

Marie chuckled, imagining Oscar The Grouch making his home in this watery mess. It seemed strangely fitting.

Another doorway came into view. A second one against the back wall, leading deeper into the house.

That was strange. From the outside, Marie had assumed the house was going to be a one room tiny affair. The roof hadn't seemed nearly large enough to accommodate a second room. But maybe more of the house was still submerged? Lake Lanier's water was absurdly cloudy. It would have been hard to see any more house, even if it was just a few inches below the water's surface.

So, assuming she had just missed something while she was outside, Marie swam across the first room, grasped the top of the second door frame, and flipped herself down, under, and through the water again, reemerging in room number two.

Somehow this room was darker than the first. The green glow of the water and the little light which leaked under the door frame was all gone now, the outside world too far away to illuminate anything anymore. Marie was relying solely and completely on her flashlight at this point.

It was hard to tell what the second room was supposed to be. Only the top third of the room was clear of the water and honestly, nothing differentiated the top third of this room from the top third of the other room. Especially in the days before ceiling fans or light fixtures. The only distinguishing feature Marie could see in this new room was the tops of a pair of picture frames, hanging to her left.

She smiled.

Picture frames could be cool. Surely the pictures within would be so faded and water damaged that there wouldn't be anything left to see, but there was no harm in looking and– oh holy cheeseballs what was that?!

The first picture frame came away from the wall easily, but Marie was shocked to see the picture inside was still mostly intact. Maybe the frame was exceptionally well made. Maybe it was airtight. But whatever the explanation, Marie saw a family stared back at her, impossibly, from behind a layer of glass.

Sort of.

Water had made its way into the frame at least partially and had grabbed the bottom half of the picture, pulled the image down, and left the whole family inside looking like their skin and clothes were melting away. The ghoulish dead black eyes of a man, woman, and child stared back at her. They looked angry. Like they were furious she had disturbed their resting place on the wall. The way the water had warped their faces, it pulled their brows down in an impossible furrow. Made their mouths hang open in the shape of ridiculous, angry screams.

Marie kicked with her feet, staying afloat as she quickly tried to hang the picture back on the nail it had hung from. She moved too quickly. Too clumsily. The old, rusted metal wire which the picture had hung from snapped and Marie dropped the picture into the water on accident instead of hanging it back up.

Well shit.

Marie looked around the room as if making sure nobody saw her mistake.

She laughed at herself. Don't be ridiculous. Creepy picture or not, she was alone here.

All alone.

Something brushed against her foot in the water. Something cold and slimy. Something moving of its own accord. Something alive.

Marie shrieked and kicked at the thing.

A fish.

Just a fish.

There were catfish all over this damn lake and that's all that was.

Marie took a deep breath, trying to remain calm.

It was time to leave.

She turned back towards the door she had swam through to get here and found it...gone.

What?

Marie shined her light all along the wall behind her, but found no evidence of a door frame.

"Maybe the water rose some. Maybe it's just under the surface here." Marie said out loud, hoping her voice and its company might keep her from panicking. Marie swam back along the wall she was sure she had come in through, feeling around in the murky water for the door frame that definitely, positively, had to be there. Right?

She made it all the way along the wall with no luck.

She turned around, started swimming back along the wall again.

Maybe she'd missed it.

That made no sense, but maybe she had missed it.

There!

Her fingers found the door frame and her heart rose back up in her chest.

She'd thought she was going crazy there for a second.

Marie let out the breath she didn't realize she had been holding, took a deep new fresh one, and submerged herself again, planning to leave the house the same way she had come in.

She went down. She pulled. She started making her way through the door, back into the first room.

The cold, slimy thing bumped into her foot again, but this time it didn't let go.

With a quick, violent jerk, Marie was tugged back into the second room, her fingers losing their grip on the door frame.

She broke the surface like a mad woman, screaming, splashing, and waving her phone's flashlight around as if it might show her what was in the water with her. She knew it wouldn't. The water was too dirty. Too full of dead fish and dead vegetation and dead kids. Too much litter from the sunken town drifted about. Lake Lanier just glowed back at her, a cloudy green haze obscuring anything and everything below Marie's waist. Her feet kicked through the water surrounded by hazards unseen.

It wasn't until Marie turned to try to find the doorway again that she saw the man in the water with her. His skin was pale white. Whiter than any skin should have been, like it had been bleached a thousand times over. His hair was sparse; nothing more than a few black strands, clinging to his soft, warped scalp. His eyes were pure black, oversized, and they appeared to be leaking down his face, his cheeks sagging, his mouth open in an enormous, gaping, silent scream.

Marie's screams, on the other hand, were anything but silent.

The lake began to rise again the next day, having claimed its share of victims for now. It would digest the bodies for as long as it needed, using them to nourish those things that lived in the depths until one day, years, decades, centuries in the future, it needed to feast again. The Lake was evil.

STORY NOTES:

Let me be clear, direct, and succinct with this story note.

Lake Lanier is evil and nobody should ever swim there again.

Lake Lanier is a real lake in Georgia, close to where I live currently. It really was created by flooding a town called Oscarville which really is a town with a grotesque history steeped in racial "cleansing" efforts, the Klan, and all the other horrors associated with 1800s/1900s America.

All of that would be creepy enough on its own.

But I got inspired to write this story when, for the hundredth year in a row, my Twitter Feed started popping up with news stories about kids disappearing around the lake. Boating accidents with people hitting trees, houses, etc. underwater which hadn't been there moments before. Catfish have grabbed children's ankles and tried to pull them under. GOD DAMN

MURDEROUS CATFISH. It's an annual tradition at this point. Summer comes? People are going to die.

Of all the cautionary tales, and all the Rational/Irrational Fears I included in this collection, I want to make it perfectly clear that this story is an imagined explanation for a fear that should be totally, completely, 100% rational.

Something is wrong with Lake Lanier.

Stay the hell away.

Peer Pressure

Kendall took the steps to Westside High two at a time, driven by some emotion which she'd been up all night struggling to identify. It wasn't anger or sadness, although it was also those. It wasn't self-loathing or disgust, although she'd puked her guts up at three in the morning, her stomach unable to take the pressure anymore. No, her eyes brimmed with tears and her throat clenched with some painful, new, unnamable feeling.

She had to find Hal. That son of a bitch.

Hal had avoided talking to her directly last night, instead opting to hide behind his phone and his few apathetic lines of text.

There had been nothing Kendall could do about it then. Her parents had taken her car keys when they saw her Calculus grade and Hal lived on the other side of town. But here at school there was nowhere for Hal to run. No faceless digital platform for him to cower behind.

Kendall didn't know what she would do when she found him. Maybe she'd slap him across the face, scream at him for wasting fifteen months of her life and then tossing her away like a used tampon.

Maybe she'd break down crying at his feet, clutching his knee and begging him to take her back.

Maybe she'd tell him that she'd do anything, anything, just to fill the Hal-shaped hole he was leaving in her heart.

Maybe she'd just kill him.

Kendall hadn't decided yet.

Whatever she landed on, whatever action best fit this nameless turmoil of emotion which propelled her, Kendall would have to make up her mind fast, because as she turned the corner from F Hall, there Hal was, with his tall, athletic frame slumped sideways against his locker. His back was to her and Hal couldn't see Kendall's approach, but she must have looked terrifying based on the way the underclassmen dove out of her way.

Kendall tried to relax.

She knew she should be cool and calm and collected here. Nobody liked a girl who blew up the way she was about to blow up. "Making a scene" in high school would get you ostracized faster than you could open the Instagram app.

Around Hal, a pink shirt started coming into view, and Kendall slowed.

There was no mistaking that shirt, that waistline, or those little tangles of blond hair which floated around them both.

Margaret Goddamn Simpson. She was leaned against the lockers just on the other side of Hal, facing him and giggling about some joke he had just told.

It froze Kendall in her tracks.

Already?

The word barred the doors to Kendall's consciousness, refusing to let any other coherent thoughts worm their way through.

Hal must have sensed Kendall behind him, smelled her perfume, the scent he claimed was his

favorite, and the one which she had worn this
morning just in case Hal gave her a second chance.
Hal turned and made eye contact with Kendall for the
briefest of instances before Kendall spun on her heel
and stormed back the opposite direction.

"Wait! Kendall! Can we talk?" he called after
her.

"Why don't you just text me," she spat back,
hoping the venom in her voice might somehow
physically hurt him. "Telling me things to my face is
too hard, isn't it?"

She didn't look back. She wanted to see if her
words stung, but looking back would make her look
weak. Other kids had lined the halls with their phones
out, hoping for a fight, but she wouldn't give them
one.

Her mind raced, trying to process all this new
information. Had Margaret really swooped in this
morning, staking her claim to the freshest meat on the
market? No. It was too fast for that. Hal had only
broken up with Kendall the night before. How could
she have known, moved in before the first period bell

even rang? No. This must have been in the works for a while. Margaret had to have been talking to Hal before all of this happened, before the text last night. Which meant that...that...

Kendall couldn't think about it. Not here in the open with everybody watching. She would cry, and if she cried and Hal didn't, then that meant he was stronger than her, and Kendall would be damned if that's how this storyline developed.

Farther down F Hall, Hal called again, trying to get Kendall to come back, to talk to him, to be reasonable.

But Kendall shut her mind down and tried to go numb; tried to race away to her safe space before her emotions got the best of her.

She almost made it.

—

Kendall slipped into B-Hall's supply closet and slammed the door behind her. She learned Freshman Year that this closet was never locked. Either the Language Arts teachers were too lazy, or the lock was broken, who knew, who cared. The B Hall supply closet was Kendall's special space to think and to cry and to scream. Whatever the day needed.

She screamed now, the white-painted concrete bricks around her reverberating her rage around and around the echo chamber of unused textbooks and safety scissors and glue.

It had been one thing for Hal to break up with her over text, but to already be hanging out with Margaret Simpson was a whole extra level. She'd known this was coming, if she was honest with herself. She'd felt Hal withdrawing for the last couple of weeks. Responding more and more slowly to her texts, liking fewer and fewer of her Instagram posts, but holy shit he didn't even have the decency to wait 24 hours before moving on to the next hot thing?

What an asshole.

What a coward.

Kendall kicked the supplies shelf to her left and heard the bin of safety scissors overhead jangle angrily.

What had she done wrong with Hal? She'd tried to be everything she was supposed to be. She spent an hour on her makeup each morning so that she would look hot for him. She went to every single one of his basketball games and cheered every time he got the ball, made a big play. She made out with him a lot. Like, a lot a lot, even when she wasn't in the mood. So what had happened? What did Margaret have that Kendall didn't have?

Kendall fell to the floor and tried her hardest not to cry. If she cried, her mascara would run, and if her mascara ran, then everybody would know she had been crying. She'd be judged for caring too much about the failed relationship.

"Why are you crying, Kendall? It was just a high school boy! There are so many others in the school. You'll find someone else. Sheesh. Get it together," they'd all say.

So Kendall took long, slow, deep breaths and tried to focus on the way her big toe was throbbing from kicking the shelf too hard.

Outside, the bell rang for 1st period to start.

Great, now she'd have to get a tardy pass. A paper slip of evidence about one more way that Kendall had failed to be good enough today.

"Damn it to hell," Kendall muttered and she turned the handle to the closet and stepped back outside, into the halls which were empty because all the other kids had made it to class on time like they were supposed to do.

—

Kendall trudged solemnly into Mr. Boyle's Calculus class a good ten minutes late and immediately she heard her classmates whispering about her.

"Was Kendall crying?"

"Look at how puffy her eyes are!"

"No, I think that's just the way she looks."

Then giggling.

Kendall tried to ignore it all as she passed Mr. Boyle her tardy slip and avoided the judgemental glare he threw her way. Mr. Boyle hated it when kids were late to his class.

"As I was saying... " Boyle said, his frustration hissing in Kendall's direction. "It's Test Day, as I'm sure you all remembered. So your desks should be clear, phones OFF and in the BOTTOM of your bags. If I see them before I have ALL tests back, then you get a ZERO and a referral." He enunciated his favorite words as if the class didn't already know exactly what was expected of them, the routine drilled into their heads since elementary school.

They all cleared their desks like good little minions, except for Kendall, who was panicking now. She'd forgotten about the test. She had been planning to study for it last night, but after Hal's text...oh, shit. Shit. SHIT. The day was going from bad to worse. Hal, then the tardy pass, now the Calculus test.

She turned back towards Mr. Boyle.

"Sir, could I-"

"No," he responded without even looking at her or caring what she was asking. He knew, of course. There was always that one kid that wanted to be the exception on test day. It just so happened that Kendall was usually that one kid.

Mr. Boyle put his head down, refusing to acknowledge Kendall further as he began to pass out bubble sheets and test packets.

Kendall sat down in her chair without calling any more attention to herself.

"...Hal broke up with her last night..." somebody, probably MacKenzie, was whispering behind Kendall.

"Oooh. So is he single then?" Aaron whispered back.

"Nah. He had his tongue down Margaret's throat already this morning."

"Margaret Jackson or Margaret Simpson?"

"Simpson."

"Yeah, that makes more sense."

Kendall squished her eyes shut and tried not to hear any more of the whispering. She tried to convince herself that she didn't care, that Hal was old news, that the faster she moved on, the better. She had bigger fish to fry for the next hour. She had to pass this Calculus test so she could get her car keys back from her parents. That was the important thing. That was the priority.

Mr. Boyle slid the test packet onto Kendall's desk as he passed, and a quick glance at the first question told Kendall she was totally fucked.

Where was the equations bank that Boyle had promised to include? She thought he was going to give them all the equations, and all she would have to do on the test was apply them correctly.

She looked up, scanned the rest of the room to see if everybody else shared her frustration.

But no, of course not, everybody else was just scribbling away as if yes, this made perfect sense, this is the way the test should look.

"Eyes on your own paper," Mr. Boyle said, suddenly materializing right behind Kendall.

"Fuck," Kendall muttered, and she knew Mr. Boyle heard her, but he didn't say anything. Just chalked the foul language up as another way Kendall was falling short.

Twenty minutes later, Erin Moon stood up, walked to the front of the class and handed her paper in, first in the class. Mr. Boyle held the scantron under the camera on his desk, smiled, and scribbled three numbers on the bottom of the page. He gave Erin a thumbs up and Erin, in return, mouthed a "Woohoo" back towards the teacher. She didn't actually say the words out loud. No, she was too perfect for that. The rules said not to talk, so Erin wouldn't talk, especially when the teacher was in the middle of reaffirming how perfect she was.

Kendall looked back down at her own answer sheet where she hadn't answered a single problem yet.

Just to get some traction, Kendall bubbled in 'C' the way you were always supposed to when you had no goddamn clue what was going on. Some study somewhere said that C was the most common correct answer, so here was Kendall's thought and prayer that researcher knew what they were talking about.

She looked over the next ten answers, found herself just as baffled by them as she had been by question one. But that made no sense. She had paid attention in class. She had a whole notebook full of highlighted, annotated, tabbed thoughts and practice problems from the past week. How had none of it stuck in her head?

She saw Hal again. Thought about studying with him late into the night last Friday night. Thought about the way he could just casually glance at her page and tell her to move a decimal over, or carry a 2. Everything had just clicked better when he was around. If only he was here now. If only Kendall hadn't done whatever she had done to drive him away.

The bell rang.

How the hell had the bell rang? Kendall had only been working on the test for...Kendall looked at the clock, which lied, saying that a whole 50 minutes had passed.

How...?

It didn't matter.

Everybody else was standing and turning their tests in and walking out the front door of the classroom, and 1st period ended the same way that it had began: With everybody else doing what they were supposed to, going with the flow to their next class, and Kendall dragging behind as society's dead weight.

Mr. Boyle cleared his throat from behind his desk and Kendall quickly just bubbled 'C' for everything that was left, rose, and hurried forward before he deducted points the way he had last time.

She considered throwing the paper directly into the trash, stealing the lighter which Kendall knew Mr. Boyle kept in his drawer for his smoke breaks behind the gym, and then lighting the entire bin on fire so that nobody got to see how poorly she had done.

But, no. Kendall fought off the impulse and passed her teacher her answer sheet, watching with dread as he held it below his document camera.

43.

Mr. Boyle scribbled the number at the bottom of Kendall's test and sighed.

"You have to start trying harder than this, Kendall," he said, as if that was some easy fix-all advice for Kendall's problems. Try harder. Just give a little extra. Find a 25th hour in the day and dedicate it to Math. Do that and you can be perfect just like Erin, just like Margaret. Be like those girls. Be perfect. Then maybe Hal will care about you.

Kendall pressed her lips together, again refusing to cry as she nodded, half to Mr. Boyle, half to herself, and walked into the hall. She needed to make it to 2nd period on time.

—

As Kendall walked past the D Hall water fountains, she kept her eyes peeled for Hal. She didn't want to talk to him, so why was she walking the same route to 2nd period that she always took? The same route she knew that Hal would be taking on his way to Language Arts? Did she want to bump into him? Was she craving that confrontation? Was she some sort of a masochist?

It didn't matter.

Because today, instead of Hal, the sweeping current of students dragged Kendall towards Margaret and her disgustingly bright pink shirt.

Margaret saw Kendall before Kendall saw her, and by the time Kendall realized they were on a collision course it was too late to change directions. The freshman around her just bumped and shoved Kendall straight into the path of the man stealer.

"Bitch," Kendall muttered, and she tried to muscle her way around Margaret without dragging the moment out any longer than it had to. But Margaret's hand whipped out and caught Kendall's shoulder.

"I'm sorry," Margaret said, and the sincerity in her voice was so genuine that it kept Kendall from slapping the shit out of her on instinct. Instead, Kendall turned, slowly, resisting the pull of the other kids around her.

Kendall took a long, slow, breath. Tried to smile so that the kids around her wouldn't think there was about to be some sort of a scene to be filmed, uploaded. No, this was just two classmates having a civil discussion in the hall. Nothing to break up the regularly scheduled class change, move along now please.

Kendall felt the lie reach her smiling lips, but it never made it to her eyes, which were already welling up with barely contained tears.

"Why?" she asked bluntly, leaving the question open-ended, letting Margaret choose how best to answer. "Why steal Hal? Why stop Kendall? Why be sorry for being better than Kendall in every way?" A thousand variations of the question hung in the open air. Take your pick, bitch. Dealers choice.

"Kendall. He's been talking to me. Trust me. You didn't do anything wrong," Margaret tried to explain. "He just...he just didn't want to have to try so hard all the time to make the relationship work. He didn't want you to have to try so hard. He saw you at all of his games, cheering him on, and he appreciates you so much. Listen to me, girl. I'm being honest here. You did nothing wrong. In fact, if you want my opinion, I think you did every single thing right. Hal just needed a change. But you're amazing and there's somebody else in this school that's going to be so lucky to date you. It just wasn't meant to be with Hal."

Kendall wanted to rip Margaret's hair from her head. She wanted to break the slut's nose for stealing her man. But Margaret was being so infuriatingly nice to Kendall about it. She was legitimately trying to make Kendall feel better after stealing Hal away? No wonder she was so popular. No wonder everybody loved her. She was so perfect.

It made Kendall hate her even more.

"Why did you have to steal him from me?"

"He wasn't happy, Kendall. You two just weren't right for each other, and I'm sorry that you're having to hear that from me, and I know that you hate me right now. I want to give you space. But if you ever want to talk about it, just give me a call. I promise to be a hundred percent honest with you about everything he told me and when and why."

A hundred percent honest? Just like Margaret was a hundred percent everything else? Smart and pretty and could play basketball with Hal and now honest also?

Kendall saw red.

She needed to walk away. Knew that was the right thing to do. She needed to walk away, to cool down before she did something rash and unbecoming. The bell was ringing, and 2nd period was starting, and the halls were empty, and Kendall was supposed to be in class with everybody else.

But when had Kendall ever managed to be where she was supposed to be before? When had she ever actually met the standards that society, her parents, her boyfriend, her peers kept piling onto her and piling onto her and piling onto her? She couldn't do it. She saw that now.

Kendall failed, like always, to measure up the way that she was supposed to.

But looking at Margaret and her bright pink shirt, Kendall had an idea. This would be the last time she ever failed. It was time to make some changes.

—

Kendall sat in the supply closet of Westfield High again, eyes clenched shut, hands pressed tight over her ears, in the hopes that she could block out the rest of the world.

Her back ached and her fingers were raw, and her cheeks were covered in salt streaks and overrun mascara. It had taken her half an hour to get her breathing back under control. She hated this place so very much. She always had. Today was just the worst. The tipping point.

How dare Mr. Boyle speak to her like that?

Like she was some dog that had dug up the back yard instead of just some kid who had forgotten to study for a calculus test. He had rubbed her 43 in her face with all the arrogance of a man rubbing that dog's nose in a piss stain on his carpet.

"Bad girl, Kendall. Bad, bad girl. You should know better. You should try harder."

God, the people around here were just the worst. From Mr. Boyle and his stupid tests that were so much harder than the practice quizzes to Hal, who had dumped her because apparently he was bored, needed a new flavor of the week, to goddamn Margaret Simpson who had swooped in and stolen Kendall's man without any semblance of a grace period.

Everybody around Kendall was just another reminder of how 'not good enough' she was. Show and tell for all the ways that proper young ladies were supposed to progress through high school, and how a proper Westfield High graduate was supposed to behave and study and excel, excel, excel, always excel.

School wasn't a place where they taught you to be successful. School was a place where you were lined up alongside your peers, then pushed and prodded and provoked until you either fit into their cookie cutter molds or until you broke, got abandoned in the trash alongside all the other dysmorphic misprints from 5th Period 3D Art.

Fuck uniqueness. Westfield High had traditions to uphold.

Kendall stood and dusted off her jeans.

Well, she would show them. She could be just as athletic as Hal, just as pompous as Mr. Boyle, just as pretty as Margaret. If society wanted her to fit in, then she'd fit in, damn it. Even if it killed her. Even if it killed them.

"This is what you wanted, world," she would say to them all as she stood before the next assembly. "This is what all of you wanted."

Kendall stepped over Margaret's body, trying but failing to avoid the blood coating the closet's floor.

Great. Now there was blood on her shoe. One more red mark to show off how "wrong" Kendall was and how she had failed in yet another way. She might as well reach down with her finger, make a 43 out of the stain to carry on the collection.

Kendall replaced the box of safety scissors on the shelf overhead as she slipped off her shoes, making sure her socks came down well clear of Margaret's mess.

She pulled the remains of Margaret's face up and over her own. The most popular girl in school's skin fit like a glove. A warm, sticky, wet glove, sure, but the proportions were perfect. The eyes were spaced exactly the right distance apart. The chin fold tucked up just under her own. It was all perfectly proportional. Perfectly Margaret.

Kendall took a slow, deep breath and turned the handle to the janitor's closet.

Now it was her turn to look perfect. To be perfect.

She licked her lips. Margarets lips.

Hal would take her back now. He would have to. Kendall would fit in now. She would make As on all her tests and it would be somehow effortless, just the way Margaret made it seem. Kendall would try harder, but at the same time she wouldn't try harder. She would simply be everything that everybody wanted her to be and it would be oh so casual. Just like it had been for Margaret.

Kendall stepped out into the hall and made it most of the way to 3rd period before the screams began

STORY NOTES:

I wrote this story for the Human Monsters anthology that Dark Matter Mag and the Nightworms are putting out together. It seemed like the perfect submission call for the story that had been itching at me for a while, and their submission guidelines did a lot to help mold and shape the idea into an end product. Peer Pressure got rejected, which is fine, whatever, the anthology is going to be kick-ass even without it. But I'm glad it gave me the push I needed to finally dive into this.

My day job is teaching High School, and if you want to see a 'Human Monster' just go walk those halls for a few days. Not my school necessarily, but ANY high school in this day and age. The amount of pressure we put these kids under when they're still vulnerable and trying to sort out their lives is incredible. To get into UGA (the big school our kids strive to) the kids are told they have to have a 4.0 GPA (be perfect). They have to have multiple extracurriculars (where they're also expected to excel. Be captain. Be President. Don't just 'be'). And then at home they're also told to work a job because it will 'build character.' You can watch as the expectations break the kids day after day. Year after year.

Kendall is fictional. Obviously. Her breaking point is overblown and dramatic. Obviously. But out of all the rest of the stories in this collection, I think this one is the most grounded in terms of character motivation. In terms of gross, horrific circumstances.

We need to treat our kids better. I guess that's what I'm driving for here.

Second Sight

Wavering blue and seafoam green lights illuminated the carnage surrounding Tyler and the top floor of Houston Medical.

Half an hour ago, Ken had gone rogue and shattered every other light source in the room.

He had believed that pure, impenetrable darkness might protect them from the beast which hunted them.

Ken had been wrong, and now Ken's mangled corpse lay on the far side of the room with bits of his bone and muscle tissue sprayed across the back wall like apple pulp ripped from a cannon.

Following Ken's death, the other four survivors abandoned the darkness theory, turned on the television, and desperately considered their next steps in the strange glow of an oceanic documentary.

15 minutes.

That was all the time Tyler had left.

Months ago, Tyler had signed up for this procedure; lured by the promise that Doctor Buck's experiment could not only restore his eyesight, but that it could actually help to enhance his vision beyond anything humans had witnessed before. Additional synthetic rods and cones had been expertly arranged throughout a prosthetic eyeball which Buck swore would revolutionize the world as they knew it.

That had been the pitch at least, and Tyler and the others they had all gone under the knife earlier that morning.

As expected, the patients had all woken up groggy and anxious to know whether or not the operation was a success.

"Your sight will come back in stages," Doctor Buck had assured them while the blindfolds were still wrapped across their faces. No need to fret if you don't see anything immediately. It will take your brain and your new eyes some time to grow acquainted with one another. Then the enhancements will kick in a bit after that."

Dr. Buck had been right.

Almost half an hour after Tyler woke up, he could see again.

It was a miracle of modern science, Tyler and the other patients all joyously agreed. Once completely blind, now the patients could see the waiting room around them. They could see their hands in front of their faces; see the white paint on the walls, see the dark tans and pale peaches of their skins.

Tyler had almost forgotten how vibrant the world was; how even the simple, straightforward décor of the doctor's office could be enough to bring him to tears.

But there was more.

The real magic began three hours after each subject opened their eyes, as their new prosthetic retinas tapped into their biotically enhanced capabilities. Pioneer signals reverberated through virgin regions of the patients' brains, and the Dr. Buck made good on his experiment's impossible promise.

Bridget had been the first patient to wake up after the surgery, and so her eyes were the first to embrace their enhancements. She had likened the experience to coming to the surface of a pond which she had only ever seen through the murky ripples of.

Now Bridget lay in the far corner of the room, bits of her femur splintered and needling through her thin-stretched skin in at least three different places. Her head hung backwards, limp, and barely still attached to her shoulders.

Her death had been horrific.

As Bridget had smiled, tears in her eyes, trying to describe the new spectrum of colors which she could see, the glass window behind her had erupted, and Bridget was lifted, shaking and screaming, about 6 feet into the air by invisible forces as her neck folded in half.

"It sees me," she had screamed in her last moments. "It sees me!"

There had been eight people in the room when the window broke. Now the shimmering blues of the oceanic documentary disoriented the only three who remained.

"Please. Send help. More people are going to die up here if you cowards don't..." Doctor Buck's voice trailed off as he listened, scowling, to somebody on the other end of his phone line. It was either somebody from the Houston City Police Department, or somebody from the Texas Bureau of Investigation, or maybe even somebody from the US Army arguing with him. It seemed like every federal official in a 30 mile radius had congregated outside the hospital, each with their thumbs up their asses, repeatedly refusing to send any aid to the top floor.

"Until we know what's up there with you, we can't risk contamination of our men; we can't risk releasing...whatever it is that's in there with you," the head of the Houston Police Department had explained nearly an hour ago on speakerphone. "If you could give us some details about what's happening, then we could run a true risk evaluation. Maybe plan some sort of a rescue. But as it is..." the Chief had rambled on and on, spouting off more and more useless excuses. Doctor Buck had kept trying to reason with them, but Tyler knew, and the Doctor knew, that they were being abandoned.

At first, nobody in the street had even believed what the Doctor was telling them.

The idea that some invisible monster was killing people on the top story of the hospital had been beyond their realm of possibility. The 9-1-1 operator had actually laughed at Doctor Buck when he told her about it.

But when Howard's pelvic bone had rocketed through the window with enough force to land seven blocks away, the police had shut their damned mouths and stopped laughing.

They still didn't understand what was happening, and they still weren't helping, but at least they were listening.

Tyler looked at Howard's corpse now, his jaw hanging askew, two holes gored into his chest as if a pair pickaxes had been driven through his ribs.

"This is it," Madeline sobbed, standing near the back wall. "I opened my eyes four hours ago. Oh god, this is it. I'm going to see that thing, and then it's going to come, and it's going to tear me apart just like it did to the others."

Madeline's hair and clothes were heavy with sweat. She had been panicking ever since Rose was impaled on the ceiling fan. Madeline knew that her time was coming next, since she had been second to last to open her eyes. She also knew that there was nothing she could do about it. She had situated herself as close to the TV as she could get, and she pressed up against the screen now, touching her nose to the image of a clownfish and watching as other streaks of purple, silver, and green darted and played somewhere off the coast of Australia.

"If I just keep my face right here, I'll never see it. And if I don't see it, then maybe it won't come after me," she whispered.

Tyler couldn't tell if Madeline was talking to him or just trying to comfort herself.

"When my eyes adjust I'll see all the vibrancy of these fishes and I'll never look away. Whatever this thing is in the room with us, it won't get angry at me. It won't. It can't. Not if I don't look at it. This can work! This can work!"

Madeline's plan wouldn't work, and she knew
it.

Her shoulders shook in spite of her
proclamations of positivity.

Donny had a similar plan two hours ago. His
grand idea was to just close his eyes and then to never
open them again. He was going to blindfold himself,
or make a helmet for himself, or something to that
effect. He'd never really gotten a chance to explain
what he was thinking. He had sneezed, and in split
second that his eyes were open, their invisible foe had
recognized him, and it had done its worst.

Tyler shifted his weight and fished his wallet
from his pocket. He opened it and, very carefully, slid
out the picture of his daughter, taking extra care to
make sure that none of the blood from the room
stained her precious face.

His daughter was smiling in the picture, which
had been taken at her second birthday party. There
was blue cake smeared across her chin, and her short
blonde hair had been pulled up in a pair of pigtails. It
had been five long years since Tyler had been able to

look at the picture. Five long years since the accident at the plant which had taken his eyesight. Tyler had been so excited by Doctor Buck's opportunity to restore his vision. He hadn't cared so much about the new, advanced nature of the prosthetics being offered. He had just wanted to see his little girl again.

Tyler had taken the picture from his pocket in the waiting room before the surgery had begun, and he had rubbed his thumb along the worn edge of the photograph the way he always did when he fantasized about seeing Lily again. Now, here, in a room painted with strangers' blood, Tyler decided that the procedure had been worth it. Even if he died right now, his daughter's perfect smile was everything he had remembered it to be.

"You cowardly sons of bitches, listen. This thing is only attacking the people who have had the surgery. They're seeing something when their eyes adjust, and that something is killing them. Unless you've somehow had the surgery which I performed exclusively on these seven, then you will be safe. But we need to get these two out of here. Now!"

To the doctor's credit, he had not abandoned his patients when the blood and the guts started hitting the walls. Before Doctor Buck even realized that he was safe up here, the man had bunkered down with his patients and done his absolute best to keep them calm. He had been the first one who realized that everybody was dying in the order that they woke up from surgery. He was also the one to find the ocean documentary on the television, and to come up with the camouflage theory.

The camouflage theory was simple enough. He proposed that whatever was attacking them was some creature which the standard human eye could not perceive, but one which the new prosthetics could. The monster, whatever it was, might live in the midst of humans every day, secure in the understanding that it was safely invisible to them, and thus, never feeling threatened. But when Bridget saw the monster, it realized that its defenses had failed it. The creature had then killed Bridget as a reaction to being seen, as a means of self-preservation. Fight had won over flight.

It was just a theory, but every death since Bridget's seemed to have reaffirmed the Doctor's suspicions. There was something in the room with the patients, somewhere, and as soon as the patients saw it, they died brutal, violent deaths at its hands...or tentacles...or claws. It was hard to say.

The Doctor screamed nonsensical rage into his phone before pitching the mobile device out the shattered window, into the night air. Doctor Buck glared at his empty hands in shock, his face pale and blue, a result of more than just the television's glare behind him.

No help was coming. Tyler took a deep breath and looked across at Madeline.

Tyler's mother had always warned him not to sit too close to the television.

"It'll burn your eyes out," she had always warned, and Tyler had, at a very young age, recognized the absurdity of the claim. Maybe it would mess his eyesight up some, but 'burning his eyes out?' How ridiculous.

Looking at Madeline, Tyler prayed that his mother might have been right. For Madeline's sake.

Tears flowed freely down Madeline's cheeks as she stared, unblinking, at an octopus which was half-crawling, half-swimming across the ocean's floor.

There were so many sea creatures who relied on camouflage to survive. A series of fish blending in with the coral, swam past the filmographer. Grouper fish hid in plain sight against the ocean's floor. There were things in this world which you weren't supposed to see, the grouper fish taunted.

Tyler checked his watch.

Madeline's eyes would adjust any moment now, which meant he himself only had about 5 minutes left.

This was it.

The end.

Tyler placed his daughter's picture carefully back in his wallet, and rose from his seat. He crossed the room and gently took Madeline's hand.

She jumped at his touch but refused to look away from the screen.

"Please. Do something," she whispered.

"I don't know what to do."

"Get a weapon. When it tries to take me, you kill it."

"How? I won't be able to see it. Not yet."

"No," Madeline "But when it's touching me, you'll be able to tell where it is. If it lifts me up, you strike behind me. If it pins me against a wall, you strike in front of me. Whatever this thing does to me, you react."

Madeline's eyes were changing; morphing from their typical baby blue to a more purple-ish color. It was the same thing everyone else's eyes had done when they adjusted.

Tyler looked at Doctor Buck, who nodded. He had seen the change in Madeline's eyes too. He had heard the plan.

Tyler bit the inside of his cheek and took a couple of steps back, looking around the room for some sort of a weapon like Madeline had suggested. There was the smashed-in table with Montres' crippled body still cratered in its collapsed plastic. Pudding cups and plastic spoons were scattered across the tile floor, and one of the table's legs hung loosely, awkwardly sideways

Tyler wrenched the leg free from the table and tested its weight in his hands. It was some sort of a light metal. Depending on the thickness of the creature's skin, the leg might be able to pierce it. Maybe. Hopefully. Tyler made his way back towards the television where Madeline was staring.

She had stopped crying and now a huge smile had consumed her face. Her cheeks were stretched as wide as they could go, and her purple eyes raced back and forth, tracking a fish as it swam through the deep blue sea.

"Can you see it?" she asked Tyler. "Can you see the colors?"

Doctor Buck had picked up a plastic chair for himself and tried to find the best place to grip the seat in order to swing it like a weapon.

"No. Not yet," Tyler admitted. "Describe it to me?"

"It's incredible," Madeline whispered. "Bridget got it wrong. It's not like seeing clearly for the first time. It's like an entire new world of experiences just opened up, waiting for us. You just...you can't even imagine. Each color is a celebration."

Madeline turned and smiled at Tyler, the love in her eyes simply glowing. It was the same look that Lily had worn on her second Christmas. The Christmas when she actually understood what was going on. Before her daddy lost his eyes.

The whole world was beauty and grace, for that one bliss-filled moment.

Madeline's head kicked backwards and a geyser of blood erupted from her nose.

"Duck!" Doctor Buck screamed as Madeline's body fell backwards, the front of her skull caved inwards as if struck by a mallet, her purple eyes splitting like eggs, with their whites mixing with the blood that poured down her cheeks.

Doctor Buck swung his chair into the open space above her collapsed body. The chair snagged, mid-arc..

Tyler thrust his table leg at the same space, but hit nothing.

"Damnit. God damnit!" Doctor Buck screamed. Tyler turned to look at him just as the Doctor's knees buckled backwards. There was a splitting noise as the bones in the Doctor's split apart and the Doctor howled in pain and rage.

"What the-"

Doctor Buck's body flew to the right like it was a golf ball being launched with a driver. The wall caved in with the doctor's impact and the entire room shook.

Buck never fell back off the wall.

Not that Tyler saw.

His bones and muscles stuck against the bricks like a bug on a windshield.

Less than a minute until Tyler's eyes were predicted to adjust.

He took a long, defeated look at the bodies and the blood surrounding him as he wandered, in a daze, towards the broken table and Montres' body.

He sat down in the middle of the pudding cups and took his wallet out again. On the far side of the room, Madeline's body twitched, but Tyler assumed - hoped, more honestly- that they were the involuntary spasms of a settling corpse and not a sign that his companion was still alive, suffering through her last remaining seconds. Tyler prayed that her last conscious moments had been spent in blissful awe of the beauty of the world instead of mangled in gruesome dismemberment.

Tyler unfolded his daughter's photo. He wanted to go out like Madeline had; staring at something unnaturally, impossibly beautiful

As he stared at his pride and joy's innocent smile, Tyler felt something shift in his eyes. His world began to focus and unfocus over and over again, as if a photographer was adjusting their lens.

This was it.

Tyler's right hand fell to his waist and his fingers brushed against one of the plastic spoons which were intended for the pudding cups.

He would never see his baby girl again after all.

Tyler grabbed the handle of the plastic spoon and, before he could stop to think about what he was doing, he swung the spoon up and into his right eye. The pain wasn't immediate, but the world went wholly, perfectly red. Tyler's left hand groped around for a second spoon, trying to find another one before the shock set in.

STORY NOTES:

Splatterpunk is a hell of a genre, huh?

I guess this story was inspired by two things really.

First: An underwhelming episode of Doctor Who. There's one story, early in Capaldi's run as the Doctor, where they're being hunted by some camouflaged alien/monster/thing. Capaldi opens the episode with this really cool monologue about how if any creature really, truly, had mastered the art of camouflage, we'd never know about it. All the creatures we've seen have some flaw in their design so that humans can pick them out. The episode devolves into some plotline that made no sense to me, but that initial premise was fun.

Fast forward to the day I learned about the Rainbow Mantis Shrimp and its 16 color receptors (as compared to our 3) and the story came together from there. A sci-fi, human experimentation story where we upgrade our vision, see one of those previously perfectly camouflaged beasts in our midst, and it gets piiiiissed.

I think this was also my first foray into just spraying as many blood and guts and bones around as possible. Both of the novels I wrote before this, and all the short stories, stayed fairly subdued as far as the carnage was concerned, so it was a blast to finally cut loose on some people.

I also want to work in an Eric LaRocca reference to say something about "What have you done today to deserve your eyes?"

Lewellyn & Co. Pest Control

"Boy, I tell you what. If I could go back 'n do it all again, I'd sure as hell change our tag line.

You know?

Llewellyn and Co. Pest Control: We'll Control Anything.

Catch phrase sounded real good on paper, huh? Only problem is, I guess we didn't quite know how much 'anything' there was out there in the wild wild world that people would want us to get controlling.

West Virginia doesn't have too much going on. Figured the weirdest thing we'd ever get called out for was maybe a snake in a tool shed. Or like, a bear wandering into town to start gobblin' up some garbage. And hell, if that's what it had been, we had enough tranqs with us to knock out an entire herd of bears. Or flock of bears. Or whatever you call 'em. We coulda pitched a bear into the back of Cletus' truck, hauled it away to the woods, and that woulda been that.

But damn. After sitting on the side of that road for seven nights in a row, not seein shit, it's was kind of hard to stay committed to the gig, ya know?

New catch phrase proposal.

Llewellyn and Co. Pest Control: We'll Control Anything You Can Actually Point Us Towards.

Cletus, the lazy sumbitch, was shifting around in his seat, and pulling his hat down a little lower until it was practically settled on his nose, and grunted his standard reply of "hunh" when I asked him if he was ready to just turn it in for the night.

Cletus was a man of few words. Not like me.

If we were ever short enough tranqs to take down our quarry, mah better half Miss Mary Margaret always joked that I could fall back on my usual plan and just talk the damn thing to death.

Way I see it, talking helps fill the hours on the job. Radio in the truck is broken, always has been, always will be, so I help fill the silence with stories about my high school years and how I met Miss Mary Margaret and anything else that pops into my head.

Since Cletus doesn't like talking much himself, sittin' around in pure silence for nine hours woulda felt like hell. My stories were just doin' us both a favor.

"Whadda ya say we just cut our losses tonight? Whatever these folks paid us to find, it ain't coming. We'll collect the nightly rate, minus the bonus for completing the job, and just move on. I got a call earlier today about some coyote that keeps comin' after Ms. Selby's chicken coop. Figure we could go pop a pup and at least walk away with SOMETHING accomplished. Just feels so stupid. Sittin' here. Parked on the side of the road. Waitin' for...what did they say? Something with 'red eyes?' How the hell are you gonna hire a pest control team to come out, take something down, without any better description of their quarry than "red eyes?" Maybe we try this. Lets drive on over to your cousin's house, grab some Mary Jane, hot box the shit out of a Raccoon, and turn it in for the ransom money. Yeah?"

I remember I chuckled and nudged Cletus in the ribs.

Cletus grunted in response.

"Hunh."

Again.

Stubborn bastard. One of these days I'll crack his shell and figure out what he'll talk back about.

But that night I was giving up. I pushed the keys into the ignition, fired Rusty up, and set my hands to 10 and 2 just like you're supposed to.

That's when Cletus yelped.

"Eyes!" I remember he shouted, finger pointing out the window towards the woods.

"Oh hey. Remember your voice?" I remember joking.

But Cletus just kept yelling. Got pretty loud. Louder than I've ever heard him get before.

"Eyes eyes eyes. You see 'em?"

I killed the engine and looked out the window like he was, but I tell you, there wasn't nothin out there. I told Cletus as much, but he wasn't hearing it. Just kept saying he saw eyes. Big red eyes.

So maybe this was finally it, right? The thing we were sent out here to collect?

So I turned to leave the truck and grabbed the handle, but Cletus grabbed my arm and said "No, no, thing was massive."

But me? I think Cletus is pulling my leg. So I climb outta the truck anyhow and get the tranquilizer gun out of the back. Cletus was supposed to get out too, but that coward locked the doors behind me. Refused to come help.

I tell you, always be careful who you hire.

But so here I am wandering into the woods like a jackass looking for something that the client never detailed, but which apparently had "red eyes."

Didn't find jack shit.

I wandered those woods for a good twenty minutes, not that I had a watch, but I swear to you it was no less than twenty minutes and there was nothing. No broken branches. No footprints in the mud (it had rained just two nights before. Ground was good and soft). But nope. Nothing.

So I got back in the truck after Cletus unlocked it and I called Cletus a dumbass and I turned the engine back on. Cletus said "Hunh," 'cause that's the only word he knows how to say, and just kept staring out his window towards where we had been pointing.

I got the car rolling without Cletus yelling this time, wheeled us back onto Birch Branch Road, and steered us back towards town.

Only, that's when things got interestin'. Cause I looked in my rearview mirror and I swear I saw those eyes Cletus was talking about. I didn't stop the truck 'cause I thought at first it was just a car following us. The glow was their brake lights. But that don't make no sense cause nobody drives with red brake lights on the front of their car. And this thing. It was following us. Kept with us all the way around a turn in the road so it wasn't just some glare comin' off somethin' or another.

I remember I nudged Cletus and told him to look back. Tell me if he saw what I saw. But 's soon as he turned around, the bastard disappeared. Like it knew Cletus was gonna look back at just that second an' it wanted to screw with me.

I turned my attention back to the road and, holy shit in God's toilet, there were those same damn eyes in the road in front of me.

I know what you're thinkin', but we were driving fast. Ain't no way no living creature just passed our car like that. But they were the same eyes, I'm tellin you.

So I didn't want to hit whatever this thing was.

I may catch varmints for a living, but I don't wanna hurt 'em. We're a humane pest control service. Bag 'em, tag 'em, relocate 'em. Preserve the sanctity of life and all that.

So yeah, I swerved to avoid the...varmint ain't quite the right word here...Varmints is small. Tiny things. And this sucker was a big ol' boy. Couldn't see him too well cause it all happened so fast, but I could tell that much at least. He was big.

So I swerved. The truck, it goes flyin' off the road. Cletus is screamin' bloody murder, but it's alright, we just hit the ditch and my fender gets a bit scuffed. Nothing Marty can't fix down at the auto shop and since he's my cousin he'll give me a decent deal, don't you worry.

But Cletus, he's not actually worried about my truck. He's turned all about, starin' back at the road. Because the thing with the eyes is gone a-freakin-gain.

About that point, I start realizing why Mayor Gammond is payin us so much for this job. Crazy ass thing with the red eyes is a sneaky sum-bitch. That's why. But even the sneakiest sum-bitch can't get the best of me.

Least. That's what I thought.

So I get out of the truck and grab my tranquilizer gun outta the bed. Cletus gets out too this time. I don't think it's cause he was feeling braver. I think it's cause he felt like a sitting duck in the truck when it was stuck in the ditch. Better to be on his own two feet where he can bolt and make a run for it.

I check back at the road and like I thought, there's no sign of the thing with the red eyes. I turn around to check what Cletus is up to, and that's when I see it. The chain link fence illuminated by our truck's headlights. Now I must have driven up and down that road a couple thousand times and I never noticed this fence. It's set back in the woods a ways. Almost like the people in charge were trying to hide it away from us. And on the fence there's this sign that says "Nuclear Plant. Keep Out."

And there's a hole in the fence.

A whole big enough for a big ol' boy that was also a sneaky sum-bitch to have snuck his way through. So I point to Cletus and I say "Giddy-Up." We've got some pests to control.

I swear. The woods on the other side of that fence stretched on forever. It got to the point where, if I wasn't the outstanding woodsman that I am, we woulda got turned around and never made it back to the truck. But as it was, even without any road or deer trail or anything else to guide us, Cletus and I found our way all the way to the big ol' concrete bunker that the fence musta been protecting.

Damn thing was covered with graffiti. I guess the local hooligans made this a hangout spot. Though, you ask me, Nuclear Power Plant is a pretty bad idea for a hangout spot. But the graffiti is sayin' stuff like

"Mothman is Real,' and 'Mothman is your DADDY now' and stuff like that. It's all misspelled. And there's this big-ole shadowy picture painted on one wall of a bird-like thing with red eyes.

"Mothman," I said to Cletus. "Like they do the festival for every year."

And Cletus just nodded.

"Mothman got red eyes?"

Again, Cletus nodded. "Hunh."

"Mothman supposed to be a big ol' boy?"

Again, Cletus nodded. "Hunh."

There was one door we could see, in the front of the bunker. The door was open and inside, I swear I could see something moving around in the dark. Like a darker, more solid black moving against the rest of the black. I stared at that doorway and I heard something scratching. Like claws against concrete. Itching against the bumpy parts.

I turned to Cletus.

Cletus turned to me.

We noped the ever living fuck right out of there.

Maybe if we were younger or stupider we might have gone in that door. Lawd knows a part of me was curious. But for $200 ain't no way in hell. No. Way. In. Hell.

So we ran back to the road and, even though I felt like something was watchin' me the whole way, we never saw those eyes again. Never saw the mothman again. I know everybody in town is gonna tell us we're crazy, but I don't care. Maybe I am. Maybe we are. But we're alive, gosh darn it. We got back to the road, grabbed everything we needed from the truck, and just started walking. We're darn lucky you pulled over and offered us a ride from town. 'Cause that feeling of being watched? It never left. Hot dang I still feel it now. Don't you, Cletus?"

Lewellyn finally...finally...stopped talking and looked over at the driver, then Cletus in the back seat.

"Hunh," was all Cletus said, though.

He said it calmly.

Sanely.

Because Cletus couldn't see the red eyes watching them through the car's back mirror.

STORY NOTES:

Rednecks vs Mothman, lets go. I figured we could use a little levity by this point in the collection.

I remember learning about Mothman for the first time at my friend Corey Austin's house in middle school. He's probably the person who got me into scary movies for the first time. 'Signs' was the big one, and I still remember that green hand reaching out from below the pantry door, the news footage which Joaqin Phoenix was watching in the closet. Swing Away, Merrill.

But the other movie we watched that stuck with me was Mothman Prophecies. Theres was just something different about it. The uncertainty surrounding the mythos was maddening for middle school me, who just wanted straight answers about the movies he was watching. Aliens- bad. Throw water on them. I could process that. But slowly losing your sanity over a Cryptid that may or may not have been real? May or may not have been warning you about Silver Bridge's impending doom? That crap got under my skin. Even though I haven't stopped thinking about the movie since I watched it, I've never revisited it. I've never wanted to. I have a feeling that, if I watched it again now, I would understand more of the subtext hidden in the film, and I would get some answers to the questions I had missed when I was younger. I don't know if I want that. Instead, leave me with my hazy recollection of the puzzle with no answer. The mystery that doesn't quite make sense. The hero. The villain. I won't get clear answers about Mothman because I don't want them. Sometimes things are better off that way.

So I guess this, my little first-person story of a story, is a bit of an ode to Corey Austin. I haven't talked to him in ages. Have no clue how to contact him. There's practically a 0% chance that he'll ever read this. But this one was for him.

Between The Lines

Patricia,

Let me begin by apologizing for the lateness of this letter. Here on the ranch

everybody is so busy rehearsing our performances and lines that it's easy to lose track of the time!

All is well. I have landed a couple of roles in local commercials and I feel like my big

screen breakthrough is just around the corner! I know that I usually write weekly, but

every day has been spent practicing and practicing and practicing. You would be proud.

Manny has been setting up meetings between me and a lot of important directors and I think

once you see me on the big screen you'll be so excited for me, and you'll understand how hard I'm working.

Maybe you remember me mentioning my friend Shauna in an earlier letter? Well,

Shauna got cast in a big production with a major studio recently. I'm not allowed to say which one, but she's

eventually going to star in a real, honest-to-God movie! It's supposed to be a romantic picture with

Ned Marshall directing (I know how much you love his movies). Manny and I are both

delighted for her, and hoping that when she does well, then maybe she could put in a good word for me.

How wonderful could it be to work on a set with such a fantastic director AND my best friend?

Eventually my breakthrough will come, I know. But I'm impatient.

Lately I've been fantasizing about what types of roles would be best for me. I know

playing a romantic lead, like Shauna, is something I've always yearned for, but

how exciting would it be to see me matching wits with a serial killer? Or stopping bank robbers?

Everyone says that 'range' is important out here.

I know those aren't your favorite types of movies, though: ones with so much death and killing.

Surely you would rather see me in a romance or a comedy, but

Kall me crazy, but I would love to shoot a gun for a scene sometime.

Imagine your little girl in an action movie: shooting the black hat off of a baddies' head

like Butch Cassidy or the Sundance Kid.

Life can be funny sometimes, can't it?

I can't think of much else that's changed in or around here since I wrote last. There is a

new girl who showed up last weekend named Holly Berkmire from South Carolina. She's sweet, but incredibly naive. I

guess that's probably how I seemed when I first showed up also, though. She thinks that if she's

uniquely pretty, then that'll be enough to land her a spot in the industry. I suppose sometimes

she's right. That sometimes actresses can skate by by out here without a lick of talent, but in most of our cases it takes hard work and suffering. So much hard work.

New girls like Holly Berkmire from South Carolina ride in every day expecting the spotlight to just...find them. But

things don't work out like that. Which is why I connected with Manny in the first place.

He promised to introduce me to the big name directors that Shauna is working with.

Eventually.

But it takes time. Patience, he keeps telling me.

And patience has always been one of my strong suits.

Remember how I saved all my pennies in order to buy my train ticket out here? How you

never wanted me to come, but I waited all of those tables and eventually managed to pay for my independence. You told me

it was a bad idea. That I didn't know what I was getting into.

How could I have known what Los Angeles was really going to be like? Well,

everything I read in those magazines was true...ish, but it turns out that you were right that I didn't have

a _full_ picture of what I was getting into. You were right that there would be bad people ready to

ruin my dreams and take advantage of a poor, lost, scared girl like me. But I'm hoping there are

some good people out here, too. People who will look past the obvious big names to recognize things like the

character and the strong work ethic which you always prided me on.

Really, I'm trying my best out here.

Early mornings and late nights. I'm reading a lot about the art of

acting and I've been watching and rewatching those old Ned

Marshall movies that we used to watch together, trying to match each actor's mannerisms perfectly.

I'm getting pretty good, if I do say so myself.

Now I guess it's time to get to the bad news of this letter though, Mama. This letter is

going to be the last one that I write for a long time, probably.

Even though Manny suggested I write these letters initially to stave off homesickness, now that I'm settled,

valuable time is wasted each night in their crafting. I hope you know that I'm happy out here

even though I'm still waiting on my big break. Manny is watching over me day and night and

rarely lets me out of his sight. I am accounted for, and so

you do not need to worry about me anymore.

Now that I'm so close with my big break, if I can just work a little harder each night, then

I am bound to land the next big role in the next big Hollywood motion picture.

Good news will be just around the corner, and I will write you when I'm able to again. For now, this

hour is better spent memorizing lines and practicing

thespian exercises with Shauna and the thirteen other girls who are here on the farm with me.

I love you, Mama.

And I know that I never said that enough when I was at home.

My crazed, teenage brain took you for granted. I know that now. But I love you dearly.

Never forget that.

Every night I sing that lullaby you taught me when I was little and I will be praying

xtra for Uncle Benny and his leg to recover and for my big break to come through soon so I can write to you again.

Take care, mama.

-Jeanine

Patricia, Jeanine's mother, finished reading her daughter's letter and folded it carefully.

A spectrum of emotions wrestled inside of her as she stared at the wrinkled white paper in her hands.

Patricia had been surprised, for a multitude of reasons, when Jeanine's first letter arrived from California a few months ago.

Firstly, Patricia had been surprised by the *means* of communication.

A letter?

From Jeanine?

Jeanine had never been one to speak her mind through pen and paper. She had always been expressive, but her modus operandi had always been strained vocal chords and slammed bedroom doors, not hand cramps and calligraphy.

A phone call would have been more in character.

Secondly, Patricia had been stunned by the first letter's arrival because Patricia had assumed Jeanine would never contact her, in any form or fashion, ever again.

Not by a phone call.

Not by a letter.

Not in a box.

Not with a fox.

Not by anything.

Not after the way things had ended between them last March; with Jeanine's black eye swelling shut as she ran away; with Patricia howling obscenities at her daughter's backside from behind the kitchen counter.

Patricia had assumed the last words she would ever say to her daughter were "get the fuck out of here," and she had worked hard to make her peace with that.

But then the first letter had arrived, and now, after weeks and weeks of receiving regular letters from Jeanine, Patricia found herself actually looking forward to the cough of the postman's old truck and each letters' arrival.

Even though she still harbored resentment about the way her daughter had moved out, the updates from her daughter out there in the big, bad world, and the idea that she was actually *making* something of herself, gave Jeanine's mother a strange pang of pride; an emotion which she thought had gone missing from her repertoire decades prior.

She had been more than ready to let her girl go the first time around, but now Jeanine's letters had reminded her just how much she truly cared for the little brat.

And now the letters were ending?

Patricia sighed and set Jeanine's apparent final letter on top of the rest which she had saved, saddened that Jeanine might disappear from her life all over again.

Emotionally whiplashed, Patricia missed the multitude of odd mistakes scattered throughout Jeanine's letters.

Maybe it was because of the years of disconnection and feeling at war with one another. Maybe it was Patricia's simple mind, never very good at puzzles. But whatever the reason: Patricia never tried to sort out the code which Jeanine had so meticulously hidden in each envelope. Each cry for help buried among the clues and the 'mistakes' which were supposed to catch Patricia's eye.

Jeanine was never one for patience.

Also, Jeanie didn't have an Uncle Benny, never mind an Uncle Benny with a leg problem.

And who the fuck was Ned Marshall?

Answers only came in November, in the form of a stranger's knock on Patricia's splintered, dust-worn Kansas front door late one evening when the sky turned its drowsy shade of peach.

"Whaddaya want?" Patricia answered the door and snapped her usual greeting.

Detective James R. Perot introduced himself and flashed his badge, uncomfortably shuffled his hat in his hands, then got straight to business.

"Ma'am do you, by any chance, have a daughter named Jeanine? Maybe a daughter named Jeanine who moved to California earlier this year?"

Patricia studied the detective up and down, really studying the man through the filter of her screen door. Perot had a thick, bushy mustache and tired, faraway eyes, any signs of optimism or carefree youthfulness ground out of them after years on the job.

"Yes," Patricia answered, judging the detective to be who he said he was. "I do have a daughter like that."

"And did this daughter write you letters?" the detective asked.

"Yes," Patricia answered again, suddenly curious about what the detective was getting after.

Why had Perot's face grown even more somber when she affirmed the letters?

They went back and forth about the letters for a few more questions while the Detective stood on the porch and squeezed the life out of the brim of his hat.

"Ma'am, did you notice anything strange about the letters? Do you still have any of the letters?" the detective asked.

Patricia eventually invited the detective into her home, pulling back the screen door, curious to understand the purpose of the man's visit. She had shown him the stack of letters which she kept carefully preserved on the top rack of her living room bookshelf.

"How do you know my daughter?" Patricia asked.

"Has she become famous, like the letters said she might?"

"Is that why you're looking into her past?"

"Is it normal for Hollywood starlets to have their humble beginnings researched and unearthed like this?"

"Would the letters get printed in Vanity Fair?"

"Is that how all the magazines learned the things that they learned about celebrities? Through surprise visits by detectives on random Thursday afternoons?"

Detective Perot didn't answer Patricia's questions immediately, which Patricia thought was rude. She had answered all of *his* questions on the spot.

Instead, the detective carefully picked up and opened the top letter from Patricia's stack.

He read through Jeanine's final letter once, twice, three times, his tired, wrinkled face growing pale as he confirmed his fears and considered how best to break the news.

Once finished, the detective folded the letter back closed and told Patricia all about Manny Rockmeir: the farmer from California who lured naive and hopeful girls to his farm through the false front of a talent agency. He promised them fame and stardom, when truly he had very different plans for them.

Patricia didn't understand why the detective was telling her about this farmer. Would he appear in the Vanity Fair article as well?

The detective sighed and continued.

Rockmeir forced the girls to write letters home as a smokescreen to keep their distant families in the dark to their loved ones' plights.

The detective explained how well the trick had worked.

How no one ever came looking for the would-be actresses before Manny dragged them, one at a time, into the barn on the back of his property. The barn which was equipped with all the tools necessary to slaughter and carve the cattle which Manny raised elsewhere on his property.

Detective Perot didn't elaborate much more than that, for the details were things he wished he could forget, but Patricia's imagination filled out the rest of the story and she screamed and shrank to the floor in a wave of understanding.

As she wailed, Perot picked up another letter, then another, then another from the pile which Patricia had saved. He looked over them while Patricia composed herself enough to stand back up and to retreat into the kitchen for a glass of water.

It was as Perot perused his fourth letter that the pattern became apparent to him.

The letter was oddly formatted and littered with unusual speech patterns, words forced into places where they didn't fit. Sentences randomly broken in two and continued on the next line.

He flipped back over to Jeanine's final letter and recognized the same pattern therein. Perot took a deep breath.

"Ma'am, may I have a piece of paper and a pen?" he asked of Patricia.

Patricia choked off her tears.

"W-w-what for?" she stammered.

But Perot couldn't answer that. Not yet.

Patricia produced a small notepad and a dull pencil, still dabbing the tears from her cheeks, and the detective began the work of picking out the first letter from each line, working his way down the left-hand side of the page slowly and writing each letter down carefully on his scratch paper. He added little slashes wherever one coded word seemed to end and another began.

The 'P' from Patricia.

The 'L' from Let me.

The 'E' from everybody.

P...L...E...A...S...E / M...O...M / S...E...N...D / H...E...L...P/..........

Perot blinked back the tears forming in his own eyes.

It was all here. If only Patricia had seen it. .

Every clue he'd needed this past year had been buried in these letters. If only he'd made the flight to Kansas sooner. But it was too good of a code. Too well hidden. Patricia didn't stand a chance of cracking it. Perot closed his eyes, trying to erase the vision of poor Jeanine Holland's flayed remains suspended from the rafters of Manny's barn.

Perot tore away his scratch paper from Patricia's notebook and tucked it into his pocket. He picked up the rest of the stack of Jeanine's letters, Patricia's last ties to her estranged daughter, and glumly proclaimed that he needed them for evidence.

The horrors encoded in their pages might help him to identify the remains of some of the other girls.

Behind him, in the kitchen, Patricia erupted in a wave of fresh tears for her daughter, unprepared for the decades of guilt which loomed before her. Detective Perot, finding no words of comfort for the broken mother, left through the screen door where he'd entered and began his long journey back to an overstuffed evidence locker in Southern California.

STORY NOTES:

You know how you always love your kids, but sometimes they do stuff that makes you absolutely hate them, even if just for a split second, before you go back to your regularly scheduled emotions?

I hate this story.

The premise was a fun one to write. A coded message, picked up by a mother who totally misses the code, and as a result she fails to save her daughter? Writing the code was fun. Writing the reveal was fun. But holy shirtballs, formatting this thing was/is a beast. Even as I'm writing this Story Note, I'm glaring at the main tab for the story wondering if I should just burn the whole thing down.

But no.

The Charles Manson parallels are too fun, and if I can just get the formatting to land, I think you will (would have, by the time you're reading this?) maybe enjoyed it. So for you, reader, I shall persist.

Pray for me. Or whatever it is you do for authors. Pour out some coffee? Whatever. I'm broken. Stupid formatting.

Pipe Dreams

Creighton stared at the pipe and tried to swallow the toad in his throat.

The pipe was narrow; barely wider than Creighton's 10-year-old shoulders, and to get through, Creighton would have to lay on his belly and crawl through the drain's muddy, slow-flowing waters.

Darren, the oldest kid in the neighborhood, was using a long, skinny stick to sweep spider webs from around the entrance while he coached Creighton up.

"You'll run into more spider webs like these as you pass through, but it's okay. We'll all pat you down and make sure no black widows or brown recluses or other six-legged freaks are on you once you come out the other side."

"Mmmh." Creighton hummed through his nervously clenched lips. Normally he would have corrected the older kid's biology, but right now Creighton's palms were sweaty with anticipation and all of his focus was being spent on not grinding his teeth together, the way that his mother always chastised him for doing.

"It's not really the spiders you need to worry about though!" Karl with a 'K' shouted excitedly from Creighton's right elbow.

"Nope! Sure isn't! Not the spiders you've gotta worry about," Carl with a 'C' echoed from his seat, legs dangling above the pipe's dark mouth.

Overhead, a car sped along the road past some skinny pine trees. Creighton saw the familiar red paint of his dad's Hyundai flicker past.

His dad was off to work, which meant Creighton's Mom was probably starting to unpack the never-ending mountains of cardboard boxes which cluttered their new home. She had spent days unloading plates and clothes and other knick-knacks, but no matter how much his mother battled the cardboard piles, there always seemed to be more boxes waiting to be turned out.

Creighton's mom and dad would be preoccupied for the rest of the day. He was all on his own, left to fend for himself amongst his new 'friends.'

Creighton had never had many friends back in Kansas. Here in Louisiana, Creighton was determined to fix that.

He would be outgoing!

He would be adventurous!

He wasn't going to wet his pants in the lunchroom, earning himself the nickname Pee Pee Preighton.

Not again.

No sir-ree. Pee Pee Preighton was dead and gone, and this was the perfect opportunity for Cool, Calm, Collected Creighton to seize the day.

He took a deep breath and turned to Karl.

"If it's not the spiders, then what should I be afraid of?" he asked, knowingly taking the other kid's bait and attempting to seem brave.

"It's little John-" Karl tried to answer, but Darren threw his spider-clearing stick at the kid's face.

Karl dove out of the way, the stick slicing a path through the air inches from Karl's ginger curls.

"It's my story to tell, dingus!" Darren shouted at Karl.

Darren composed himself and turned towards Creighton, smiling. But his smile didn't seem nice or happy to Creighton. Instead, it looked evil; like Darren was waiting to do something cruel.

"You have to hear the story before you go through the pipe. Its a safety thing. Just so that you know what to do if... he... shows up."

The other boys giggled and nudged each other with their elbows. Creighton scrunched his eyes and studied Darren's face, looking for signs that the older boy was just kidding around. But Darren's face was deadly serious.

"...who is he?" Creighton asked.

"Johnny McGowan." Darren whispered the name like it was a secret, just barely loud enough for Creighton to hear. The other boys all gasped collectively and looked towards the darkened entrance to the pipe as if they expected to see something, or somebody, looking back at them from the darkness.

Now, Creighton was not a dumb kid. He knew when he was getting played, and Creighton knew that Darren and the neighborhood kids were undoubtedly playing some sort of a prank on him.

None of the other kids were good actors.

Their fake shock and fear about Johnny McGowan was pitifully obvious, but Creighton decided to play along. He needed these kids to like him. He needed to seem like he was fun and brave. Whatever they were about to tell him, or whatever they were going to make him do, Creighton needed to just be cool about it.

"Who is Johnny McGowan?" he asked like the other kids expected him to.

"He lived just up the street in...wait, what house did you move into, Creighton?"

"The one with the blue shutters."

"Holy shit, dude. Same house. Johnny lived in that same house!"

The other kids began to murmur excitedly with one another, and Creighton heard 'Carl with a C' make a five dollar bet with Jose that Creighton wouldn't "actually do it."

Whatever that meant.

Creighton drew his shoulders back, puffed his chest out, and made sure he was standing up straight.

"That's crazy. Same house. But anyway," Darren continued. "Johnny was down here playing in this creek last summer when he heard a cat in the pipe. None of the rest of us heard the cat, but Johnny insisted that he heard one in there. So he crawled in, to try to save the cat." Darren was staring straight at Creighton, his eyes boring into Creighton's soul, daring him to look away. Creighton met his eyes and tried not to look nervous.

"But Johnny never came back out. While he was in there, the water level rose. My dad said that the police said that he got all the way to the middle of the pipe before he drowned, unable to get back out. They had to bring in a firetruck to get his corpse out. They did CPR for over an hour, but there was nothing they could do to save him."

Creighton wanted to object. He wanted to point out to Darren that there was no way that was true, because that's not how things really worked, but he bit his tongue instead.

"Poor Johnny," Karl with a K said, and he wiped away a fake tear.

Creighton took a deep breath and looked back towards the pipe.

"So, what does that have to do with me?" he asked, staring at the murky water that spilled from the pipe. It really didn't look that dangerous. The water that he could see was four, maybe five inches deep, and it had to be like that all the way through the pipe, right? There was no way a kid had drowned in water that deep. The other kids were just trying to scare him, that was all.

"Well," Darren said. "Even though they got his body out, me and the boys still hear him every now and then. When the sun is setting, and the wind is just right, we'll hear Johnny calling out to us. Asking us to come into the pipe to play with him. He says he's lonely. So lonely. And he wants one of us to come play with him...forever."

Darren's smile deepened; his lips cutting a sinister path through his cheeks, his eyes glittering with an energy that was even more unsettling than Darren's story had been.

Creighton kept studying the entrance to the pipe.

No, the water wasn't super deep, but the sides of the pipe were narrow. Creighton wasn't sure how he would be able to move once he was inside the pipe and, ghost or no ghost, the idea of getting stuck in the darkness was disturbing. He tried to brush away the thought of the pipe collapsing, with him in it, his Dad's red Hyundai driving up later and falling in and crushing him along with the pile of asphalt, soil, and roots.

"No big deal," Creighton said. "I'll go play with your dead friend." Creighton shrugged, nonchalantly, hoping that the gesture would hide the way that his hands had begun to shake.

The other boys jumped up and down and hooted and hollered. Karl with a K immediately ran up the dirt embankment, crossing the road without looking both ways, and dropping down to look through the other side of the pipe.

"We're all clear over here!" he shouted, his voice echoing down the metal passage.

Darren clamped a hand on Creighton's shoulder.

"Cool, man. Cool. So. Here's how this'll go. Karl's on the other side of the pipe there. I'll go join him and we'll make sure nothing crazy is happening, and we'll help pull you out the other side once you get there. Carl and Jose will stay over here, and they'll help pull you out this end if anything goes wrong in the beginning. If you make it all the way through the pipe, then you'll be part of the gang. We'll tell you the password to the tree fort and everything."

"Hey! The tree fort isn't-" Jose started to say, but Darren raised his hand to silence the younger kid. He and Jose stared at each other for a moment before Jose backed down from whatever stance he was taking.

"You make it through, and you're getting the password to the tree fort," Darren reasserted. "No question about it. But you have to promise us all one thing."

"Sure," Creighton said. "Anything."

"If you hear Johnny in the tunnel, you have to get the hell out of there. As fast as you can. When he calls to us, he sounds...angry sometimes. I don't want to know what he would do to us if he caught one of us."

Creighton frowned and nodded.

"If I hear Johnny, I'll get out."

Darren slapped Creighton on the shoulder, nodded at him, and then chased Karl across the road to the far side. Creighton took a deep breath and gripped the edge of the pipe.

"Wait!" Jose shouted.

Creighton turned, and Jose handed Creighton the stick which Darren had been using to clean the entrance earlier.

"Bring this. To help with the spider webs," Jose said.

Creighton smiled in appreciation and accepted the stick. Then, before he could psych himself out, Creighton lowered his head and pushed his shoulders into the pipe.

Immediately, the darkness swallowed him. The other end of the pipe, on the far side of the road, looked like a tiny white pinprick of a star ten thousand miles away. Creighton pushed forward and lifted his feet and knees into the pipe along with the rest of his body, then tried to orient himself to some position suitable for crawling.

It was harder than he had expected.

There was barely enough room for his arms to get around his sides, and Creighton wriggled back and forth, forcing his hands up, past his face, and orienting himself like he was diving into a pool. He rattled the stick around ahead of himself, clattering it against the sides of the pipe to break up any spider webs before he rolled his shoulders and pushed with his toes, inching his body farther into the pipe.

Creighton gasped and strained his neck, struggling to keep his chin above the water. With his body oriented the way that it was, and Creighton essentially slithering along the pipe like a snake, it was harder than he had expected to keep his mouth clear of the shallow, grimy drainage.

It's no surprise Johnny drowned down here, Creighton thought. The water didn't look this deep from the outside.

But Creighton tried his best to cast off the morbid idea.

Johnny wasn't real. The other kids had just been trying to scare him.

"How you doing in there?" Darren called from the far end of the pipe.

"Great. It's just hard to move."

"Try moving like an inch worm. Bring your knees up to your stomach, then push forward with your feet! That's how Jose made it through!"

Creighton dropped the stick which was weighing him down and tried the suggestion. He edged himself forward a little bit, scraping his elbow, but making recognizably more progress than his shimmying had been making previously.

"Yeah! That's better." Creighton called back.

Creighton shut his eyes and just focused on his inching motion for a few minutes, slosh, slosh, sloshing his way through a spiderweb and descending deeper into the pipe. Twice, he moved to fast, and muddy water splashed into his face, coating his lips and flooding his nostrils, and he had to stop to cough and snot-rocket the sludge out.

"You okay?" Darren called at the sounds of Creighton's discomfort.

"Just fine," Creighton responded, more water entering his mouth as he replied. He spit in front of him, feeling the grit of the mud catching on his teeth. His clothes were going to be absolutely soaked after this. Creighton wondered how he was going to explain his ruined shirt, pants, socks, and shoes to his mother when she asked. He hadn't thought about that yet.

There was a rushing sound, like waves lapping onto the edge of a sandy beach, and a large gush of water hit Creighton in the face.

He hadn't been moving that time.

The water wasn't coming from his own splashing. His eyes flew back open, and he looked around wildly.

What had that been?

"Guys! Did you do that?" he called in between coughs.

"Do what?" came the reply from Darren's end of the pipe.

"There was just a wave. Like somebody splashed water in my face. I don't know..."

There was silence from the far end of the pipe.

"Darren?"

No response.

"Guys!?"

Still no response.

Creighton began to hyperventilate. He looked up tried to locate the light at the end of the tunnel. It was still there, but it appeared just as impossibly distant as it had seemed originally.

Creighton had to go back. Maybe the other kids would call him a sissy, but he wasn't about to drown down here in the pipe. Pee Pee Preighton lived a sad existence, but at least he lived. Creighton would find a different way to impress his new friends.

Creighton tried to backtrack through the pipe, tried retreating in the direction he had come, but he couldn't figure out how. His hands couldn't find anything to push against in the slick mud. His knees slid around uselessly, and he bumped his head against the top of the pipe.

Was the water getting higher?

Creighton pressed his lips together tightly, trying to block out the water that suddenly covered his mouth. He could still breathe through his nose, but if the water rose another inch...

Panic set in. His heart began to race and the toad reemerged in his throat.

Creighton began to inch-worm his way forward through the pipe as quickly as possible, not daring to cry for help, lest more pipe water rush into his open mouth to try to drown him. He had to pause in between motions to let the water settle back down. He took short, quick breaths through his nose in between the assault of the sloshing drainage. In those moments when Creighton was still, he began to hear the voice.

"Do you...want to...play?" the whispers echoed up and down the pipe, and Creighton noticed a second set of splashing sounds, coming up behind him in the pipe.

Tears poured from Creighton's eyes. This was horrible. Why had he agreed to do this?

He tried to find ways to move faster, rolling onto his side so that half of his mouth was under water, the other half above water, trying to only breathe through the edge of his mouth as he pressed his hand against the pipe in front of him and pressed his back against the opposite side. He was able to get some traction this way and worked his way deeper and deeper into through the tunnel.

And still the water rose.

Creighton was going to die down here.

They were going to have to send in the fire department, just like they had with Johnny, and they were going to have to drag his bloated corpse out for his parents to see.

Creighton couldn't breathe, not from the water anymore, but from his own terror. His breaths came exclusively in short, quick, bursts, and Creighton began to feel dizzy. The sounds of Johnny McGowan's pursuit had caught up to Creighton now. The splashes of the dead boy sounded thunderous in the cramped, narrow pipe way.

Something brushed up against Creighton's toes. Something cold and wriggling.

A hand?

Fingers?

They grabbed at him through the darkness.

Creighton whimpered and kicked backwards as hard as he could.

GET AWAY, JOHNNY! I DON'T WANT TO PLAY WITH YOU. I DON'T WANT TO PLAY WITH ANYBODY ANYMORE. I JUST WANT TO GO HOME. Creighton thought the words as 'loudly' as he could, screaming internally without daring to open his mouth to form the words.

His kick connected with the thing behind him. Creighton felt something crunch beneath his heel, and the searching fingers which had been grabbing at his ankles fell away.

There was a final splash, and the thing stopped chasing him. Creighton hoped that was the end of it.

Then the temperature dropped, and Creighton heard a low croaking sound reverberate through the pipe. The muddy drain water rose and swelled even higher around Creighton, and somehow the tunnel grew darker, as if somebody had dimmed the lights.

Creighton looked up, 'above' himself, to try to find the light at the end of the tunnel.

It was gone.

Creighton was lost to the pipe.

In one final, desperate attempt to save himself from a watery grave, Creighton plunged his entire face into the drainage water and inched forward, like Darren had told him to, desperately, frantically thrashing around without any care about the damage the pipe was doing to his hands or his knees, or his face. He just wanted to get out.

Two hands grabbed Creighton's shoulders, and Creighton felt his body get jerked forward.

The water fell away, and open air slapped Creighton in the face. He gasped, taking deep, full breaths, blinking rapidly, and trying to get his vision to return in the sudden blinding light of day.

All around him, Creighton heard the other boys laughing.

"Holy shit! Creighton, you weren't supposed to shove your face in the water like that!" he heard Karl saying.

"Yeah, seriously, man. Not smart. If we hadn't been able to reach you, you might've actually drowned in there! We would've had a Johnny McGowan for real," Jose said. He wasn't laughing nearly as hard as the other boys were. In fact, his face looked terrified, ashen, and pale.

"You did well," Darren said, his hands still firmly gripping Creighton's shoulders. "You okay?"

Creighton nodded, but dropped his eyes towards the ground. He wondered if the other boys could tell he had been crying through his face full of mud.

Jose began slapping at Creighton's clothes, searching for spiders as promised, while behind

Creighton, 'Karl with a K' walked around to the mouth of the pipe. Creighton heard his "friend's" voice echo down into the pipe which had so nearly killed him.

"Hey, Carl! Come on out, dude. You scared him good! You should see the new kid's face right now!"

There was no response.

Creighton blew pipe water from his nose and spit a glob of brownish green goop into the leaves beside his foot.

"Carl? Come on out, buddy." 'Karl with a K' called a second time.

Creighton turned around and crouched to look back into the pipe. The long, dark passageway with the miniscule pinprick of light at its end smiled back at Creighton, empty.

Carl was nowhere to be seen.

"Carl?" Darren questioned.

The fear in the older boy's voice seemed genuine this time, and he stared, disbelieving into the open mouth of the pipe. But nothing responded to

Darren. Nothing moved in the darkness except the black widows and the brown recluses, and the muddy flowed, apathetically, as if nothing had ever happened.

STORY NOTES:

Hey check it out. Another story based on real life stuff.

The pipe is real. But unlike with Lake Lanier which is truly evil and needs to be killed, the pipe is just a pipe. When I ran cross country in high school, the big hazing ritual was pulling over on our runs and having the Freshmen crawl through the pipe. Don't get me wrong, hazing rituals are bad. But as far as all the high school hazing rituals I've heard about, the pipe was pretty tame. You crawled through the darkness for a second, got a bit muddy, and then you were done. Wallah.

But despite how plain and straightforward "getting piped" was, there was a moment in the pipe where it got truly dark. Where paranoia set in and you just had to kind of wonder, right? How vulnerable were you in that moment, army crawling through a tight space with absolutely no way to speed up if something started to go wrong. If the seniors had been assholes, cruel, broken human beings, they could have plugged the ends of the pipe and left us for dead and there would have been literally nothing we could have done about it.

So Pipe Dreams was me trying to relay that idea of claustrophobia. Of childhood fears and the desperate ends we're willing to go to, sometimes, in order to make friends when growing up. Sprinkle in some supernatural mumbo jumbo for good measure and we've got a horror story :)

Bad Touch Beach

I sit on the edge of my towel and stare at the hole in the sand where Conrad was just standing.

To my left, Kylie is screaming.

She has positioned herself in the dead center of her towel, eyes racing around as she watches odd clumps of 'whatever just grabbed Connor' circling around her.

It is hard to tell what, exactly, these things are.

They're doing a fantastic job of staying just below the beach's surface, shielded from view by a thick, fine layer of Stillwater Beach's famously white, small-grained sand. I'm desperate for the sand to fall away; desperate for a second look at our attackers, because what I think I saw the first time makes no sense.

I was only able to see Conrad's killer for an instant.

A split second.

But I could have sworn that what grabbed him were hands.

Old, dried out, decrepit looking hands which rose, impossibly, up from underground.

Human-esque in their shape, with raw, red knuckles and digits and fingernails protruding from the ends of their fingers which wrapped themselves around Conrad's throat and snapped his neck like a glow stick.

But that couldn't have been what I saw, because that makes no sense.

How the hell would human hands move below the surface of a sandy beach like this?

So I'm staring at the little lumps of displaced sand, hoping for another look at what these things are, wondering what Connor unearthed in his stupid hole.

I had whiplash from the way the afternoon had turned so quickly, so violently.

One moment Conrad had been drunkenly "digging a hole to China," chugging his way through beer number six, and making eyes at Kylie. Then the next second he had been pulled...where?

Under, obviously.

But under to *where*?

My head is spinning. The big picture of what's happening to us is too much to consider in too short of a time.

And Kylie won't stop screaming.

But yes. They had to be hands.

Logic be damned, that's what I saw grab Conrad.

Human hands emerging from the sands.

My own beer still lingers in my left hand, half-crushed from the way I squeezed it in my surprise. The waves crashing in the background provide a repetitive, rhythmic percussion, a steady bass line to accompany the high-snare drum roll of my heart rattling in my chest.

"Oh my god, they're all going towards Kylie," Jeanette cries from her position atop a reclined beach chair.

I look to my left and Jeanette is right.

The lumps of displaced sand which mark the hands' locations have been spiraling the abandoned beach somewhat, but now they are moving in a flock towards where Kylie crouches, hyperventilating.

I watch the lumps progress with a morbid curiosity.

Every now and then a lump bumps into a shell. The shell rolls away and the tan, cracked flesh of the fingers gets exposed, only for a moment, to the open air. The sight confirms my fears. It convinces me that I'm not crazy, but there really are fingers worming their way across the beach.

Then, just as quickly as when they grabbed Conrad, the fingers slip back under the pearl-white surface of Stillwater Beach.

Watching the hands move beneath the surface of the beach's sand reminds me of a farmer plowing a field, just from the bottom up instead of the top down. The ridges which the hands' movements are producing are only three, four inches high, but the impression is unmistakable. Those ridges are just the tip of the iceberg. Whatever is under the sand is big. Hidden. But big.

I see the finger-sized lumps of sand congregate around Kylie's towel, but they don't expose themselves to the open air. Not willingly. They begin to poke and to prod at the bottom of Kylie's towel, and Kylie yelps in surprise as one jabs her in the heel.

"Somebody *help*" she shrieks again, her big brown eyes aimed, pointedly, right at me.

I avert my gaze.

What could I do?

Kylie's words echo up and down the beach, but there is nobody to hear them besides us. There are no life guards. No other tourists. Shit, there weren't even any seagulls in the air.

We had come to this beach for isolation. We had gotten it.

"Hold on, Kylie. I'm going to see if I can get closer to you," Jeanette says a few feet behind me. She shifts her weight around on her beach chair, stepping onto the 'seat' part of the structure and lifting the 'back' part of the structure in front of her. She grips the chair's back like it's a set of handlebars and her eyes scan the sand below her frantically.

"Hurry!" Kylie screamed as another finger prods her through the bottom of the blanket.

Jeanette jumps straight up. While her body weight is suspended in mid-air, she uses her handhold to jerk the chair forward beneath her. It slides it a few inches forward on the sand before Jeanette lands, safe again on the seat.

"Careful!" I shout, and I glanced back towards the hole where Conrad had disappeared.

His beer can is still lying on its side, right beside the hole which he had been digging. The last of the beer has spilled out and the ground below is already drying; moisture unable to survive for long in the oppressive July heat.

One of the finger-lumps from the side had investigated the beer can earlier, bumping it and spilling beer onto a shell,

Whatever these things in the sand are, they aren't interested in aluminum, like a beer can. Or cloth, like a beach towel. Or plastic, like the legs of Jeanette's chair.

They apparently only want skin.

Flesh.

More of them have been showing up each minute since Conrad went under. I wonder if they're like sharks. If they can smell blood on the sand like a Great White can smell sand in water. There were at least fifteen different lumps rushing around through the sand now. A school of sharks, like a school of fish. Is that what shark groups were called? Schools? Seems too civilized.

I tuck my knees closer to my chest and make sure that my toes are far away from the edge of my blanket. To get to me, the hands will have to reach up and over the edge of the blanket. They'll have to expose themselves to the open air, which they don't seem to want to do. They have bumped the edge of my towel a couple of times. I have felt them wriggling against my ass, through the towel. But they haven't made a move on me yet. Or on Kylie. Or on Jeanette. I have to assume the open air is what's keeping them at bay.

Don't.

Touch.

The.

Sand.

Don't give them easy access to my skin.

It seems simple enough.

I look behind me, towards the high dunes and the cattails which separated our beach from the Jeep which we rented for the weekend.

How fast are these things, I wonder.

Could I make a break for it while they are all distracted by Kylie?

Maybe.

But I shook the thought away.

I'm not going to seriously consider abandoning my friend. I'm not that kind of a person; not a coward.

Am I?

Jeanette has made good progress towards Kylie by now. She had developed a rhythm of hopping, sliding, and landing which was slow, but efficient.

Kylie had noticed this, and had stopped screaming quite as loudly.

"Come on, Jeanette. Come on. You can make it. Help me."

But now I'm realizing that I'm confused about what the plan is.

Even once Jeanette reaches Kylie, what is that going to help?

They would be together, sure. But they would still be stranded and surrounded. It wouldn't be any easier to shuffle-hop with *two* people on the chair, would it? Was there something I was missing?

It didn't matter. I would never have to find out.

Just as I'm thinking this, there is a loud ripping noise, and Jeanette's feet break through the cheap plastic bottom of her seat.

There is no time between Jeanette's feet hitting the sand and a hand emerging to latch onto her.

I get a better look at this hand than I got 'Conrad's' hand.

It is clearly human. There's no mistaking it. The hand's skin is dry and scabby and its ancient, chipped fingernails dig into the flesh of Jeanette's foot.

Jeanette has just enough time to scream before another hand leaps from below and grabs at her opposite leg. The second attacker's nails rake at Jeanette's calf muscle, shredding it with ease and sending a cascade of sticky crimson blood splashing across the sands of Stillwater.

From there, it becomes a feeding frenzy.

Jeanette stumbles, unable to support herself on her left leg. Her elbow hits the sand and two of the bulges which had been harassing Kylie closed the gap to her exposed flesh in an instant. It was like watching starved piranhas being fed at an aquarium.

I look away as Kylie screams.

When I choke down my vomit and work up the urge to look back, there is nothing left of Jeanette except for a large, wide red puddle sinking slowly into the sands.

The lumps vanish for a moment. They disappear along with Jeanette's bones and muscles, lost below the surface of the beach.

I have the ignorant thought that maybe they are gone. Maybe between Conrad and Jeanette, these mysterious hands have had their fill.

But the lumps reemerge, swarming back towards Kylie to continue encouraging her away from her blanket.

Can they tell that she's the weaker of the two of us? Can they tell that she's more likely to freak out, to lash out at them, to expose herself?

Or am I sitting still enough, quiet enough, to avoid detection. Maybe this is a vibrations in the sand, sort of a scenario. Conrad was digging, Jeanette was hopping, and Kylie is screaming. Maybe that's what's drawing their attention. Maybe if I can just sit here perfectly, unnoticeably still, then they'll forget about me.

I slowly look, turning nothing but my head, from Kylie, to the hole where Conrad had disappeared, to the puddle where Jeanette had died, and back towards the Jeep.

I can just see the rim of the Jeep's roof from here.

I weigh my options.

I'm fast. Well, I'm comparatively fast. I'm the third string wide receiver for our high school. Granted, it isn't a very big school. I'm not too proud to admit that. And granted, there is a big talent gap between myself and the Fightin Buzzards' other, better, options at the position.

But still.

All those summer practices in blistering, 100 degree heat had to count for something, didn't they?

I begin to wonder if I can make it. Not that I'm going to try. I'm not going to abandon Kylie like that.

I'm not a coward.

But still.

I wonder.

"Hey!" Kylie shrieks, as if able to sense where my thoughts are wandering.

I snap back to attention and, in an inexplicable act of desperation, I throw my empty beer can at one of the sandy lumps which hides the cannibal fingers.

The can flies straight and true, making a clunking sound as it bonks the sandy protrusion.

The lump turns, bumps the can back, and then shifts back towards Kylie, apparently uninterested, the same way that the fingers had previously been uninterested in *Conrad's* widowed beer.

Score one for consistency.

I'm learning everything I can about these things. Scientific method, bitches. Hypothesize, test, measure, repeat.

I wonder if the sand hands would be interested in my sandals if I threw them. They smell like me. But hands can't smell. Can they? Which leads me to consider the question: how are they distinguishing between flesh and these other materials, anyway? How do they know what to attack?

"Hey!" Kylie shrieks once again, and it's clear that she expects me to do something.

Scientific progress will have to wait.

"What?" I respond, and Kylie looks at me with the widest, angriest, most what-the-fuckiest eyes I've ever seen. She gestures at the twenty-ish sand ridges which are circling around her.

"Help!" she says, as if there's some clear, obvious way for me to assist her.

"What do you want me to do?"

"I don't know! Anything! They're leaving you alone!"

And that's true

...was true...

But now that I've started yelling, there are some ridges popping up closer to me than to Kylie. The vibrations theory wins a point in my mind. Damnit. If only I'd stayed quiet like I had intended.

"Get over here!" Kylie pleads.

"What would that help?"

Kylie doesn't have an answer for that, so she just screams incoherently at the sky.

We stay like that for hours. I don't know that for sure. It might not have been hours. I don't wear a watch. But however long we stayed like that: it felt like a goddamn eternity, and the sunburn on my arm got at least five shades darker, devolving from a normal pinkish hue to a cherry-red, rash-like monstrosity.

I have to get out of here.

I reach down below me and drag the back end of the towel forward, bunching the towel up near its middle around my feet.

A handful of the sandy lumps divert their attention back towards me, come up, and bump against the edge of the towel before rolling backwards again.

I hold my breath until they seem to have lost interest and then straighten the towel back out, unbunching the fabric around my feet and stretching the towel forwards a few inches closer to our Jeep than it had been originally.

Again, the fingers in the sand come to investigate, and again the retreat after brushing the fabric and deciding that it wasn't skin.

I let out a breath which I hadn't realized I was holding in.

It will be slow moving, but I believe I can inch-worm my safe haven all the way back to the Jeep. Maybe even before night falls, if I'm lucky.

Kylie sees what I'm doing and begins to shout my name.

God, the girl can not shut up, can she?

The fingers in the sand all turn their attention back towards her, bristling with desire at the sound of her screams.

"Are you going back to the Jeep?" she shouts.

I nod my head, but I don't open my mouth, because I'm not stupid.

"Hold on. I'm coming too."

Kylie reaches down and tries to copy my inchworming movement, bunching up the back of her towel and then sliding the front portion forwards.

She loses her balance.

Her hips and her shoulders wobble dangerously back and forth, and I imagine I can see the fingers in the sand holding their breaths with anticipation.

But Kylie catches herself.

She stands back up on shaky knees and screams for the hundredth time.

The fingers resume their restless swimming, frustrated and hungry.

I go back to my own inching routine, feeling bad about being a little disappointed that Kylie caught herself. I've never liked Kylie. Conrad always made her tag along to things because he thought she was hot, but now that Conrad is gone, I don't care about her and her screams are drilling a hole through my brain. I would never wish harm to come to a person. But if harm came to Conrad, and if harm came to Jeanette, then it only made sense that it should come to Kylie also.

She seemed to be desperate for death. Otherwise why would she still be screaming?

I inch my towel forward once. Pause. Wait for the cannibal fingers to lose interest. Inch forward again. I repeat this process over and over and over. And then I repeat it over again.

By the time I reach the dunes that mark the edge of the beach, the fingers seem to have lost interest in me. They recognize that I have a pattern. They recognize that I can balance. That I'm level-headed and cool. And so they stop waiting for me to make a mistake. They stop monitoring me and all - Jesus, there must be at least a hundred of them now- turn to watch Kylie.

Kylie is moving much slower than I am. She has almost lost her balance three times and she keeps stopping and sitting down on her towel to recompose herself.

She says that she's feeling dizzy and lightheaded.

That makes sense.

She hasn't been hydrating at all so far this trip. Cherry flavored vodka doesn't exactly help with your endurance. I look back towards the hole where Conrad disappeared. The cooler is still over there.

There should be at least one water bottle in it. But it's too far away to matter now.

I look back at Kylie.

She's gone pale. Her eyes are lolling about in her head uneven, unfocused. I see her right arm starting to tremble, unable to hold her body up in its odd almost-crawling position. This is it. She's going down.

"Kylie!" I shout because I'm supposed to. But she doesn't seem to hear me. Even if she could hear me, what good would that have done?

I brace myself for what is about to happen.

I think I'm ready to see the hands again. I'm ready to bear witness to my adversary. Maybe I'll notice something this time which gives me an edge against them. I already know enough to beat them; to escape; to reach the car unharmed, but I'm curious to know more.

I'm ready for them when Kylie topples backwards, her whole back slapping against the white sand at once.

153

It turns out that I'm not ready for them.

When the hands take Kylie, they don't just eek past the surface of the sand this time. Oh, no. We're past that now, apparently.

The fingers emerge first. I see hundreds of them press up from beneath Kylie as if she's being raised on a bed of nails. Then the hands come through, tanned and ruinous just like before.

But the arms.

My god, the arms.

They're more like a crab's appendages than a human's. They're long. They're powerful. They're hinged with thick, bulbous joints that would have to be cracked by a hundred pound lobster cracker.

Kylie's body gets raised into the air by the arms five, ten, fifteen feet, and she's too tired to scream anymore. The things from the sand hold her up towards the sun like an offering before latching onto her every grabbable protrusion and pulling her apart.

There is a ripping sound and Kylie pops like a balloon.

More hands rise up from the sand to catch the bits of bone and innards which are cascading from above. Each hand seizes its bit of the loot, then retreats back away from the open air. They bring parts of Kylie down to their mouths-whatever those look like, safely hidden in the cool, wet Earth.

The longest crab-arms -the ones which ripped Kylie open- shake her decapitated head and her limbs to jiggle a little bit more gore loose for the feast below. The other hands stay low, near the sand, thankful for the offerings which the higher fingers libate to them.

I watch the show for longer than I should. It's fascinating in ways that I cannot appropriately describe. I feel like I am watching something religious; something holy. It's as if the proceedings before me are more than just a feeding frenzy; more than wolves at a slaughter. No. There's a sense of camaraderie here. An almost communist atmosphere, with the longer, stronger arms taking care to feed bits of Kylie to the little ones below. Are these hands a family? A pack of lions hunting and feeding together?

Passing food down to the cubs? Or are all of these arms connected to one body down below, working more like pinkies and thumbs, appendages with different strengths, different purposes? What is coordinating this communion? Mutual respect? The bonds of fraternity? Or is this simply one being using its resources effectively?

I long to see what lies below the sand's surface.

I stay there, at the edge of the dunes and the grassy reeds for longer than I should have. I should have made my escape while the arms were preoccupied. I should have taken advantage of Kylie's death to make some more headway towards the Jeep.

I can see the Jeep now. Fully. Clearly. Whereas before I could only see its roof: now it sits before me, a chariot to safety. Huge rubber tires ready to create a foot of separation between myself and this (these?) insatiable sand-monsters.

The longest of the crab-arms withdraws back into the sand once more, leaving bloody streaks of Kylie behind to mark its point of emergence. Kylie's towel is covered in sand now, awkwardly folded over on itself from when the hands burst forth.

I begin to inch the towel forwards again.

I wonder, for a moment, if the fingers might stop pursuing me once I reach the reeds. Maybe the vegetation will create some sort of a natural barrier to stop their pursuit of me. Maybe I have reached my sanctuary at last.

But then one set of reeds gets jerked below the sand's surface. Then another. Then another. Whatever protection they might have afforded me, the fingers in the sand are removing them; pruning the vegetation to give themselves easy access to me.

I commit myself to reaching the Jeep once again. I work slowly.

I inch my towel forward once. Pause. Wait for the cannibal fingers to lose interest. Inch forward again. But here's the problem. Now that I'm the only person left on the beach, the fingers aren't losing interest anymore. They're surrounding me, trailing me, watching over me with an attention that is unwavering and unflinching.

I miss Kylie.

I try to focus on the way that I'm shimmying my towel forward, but I'm distracted by my curiosity.

I'm watching the sand mounds circle me, trying to notice something, anything, about them which can clue me into what they really are.

If these are all parts of one larger being, I try to imagine the monster waiting below me. I imagine the complexity of the creature, with so many limbs coordinated to drag its prey down. How far? Just below the surface? Or is my predator deep underground, past the crusts of the Cretaceous and the Jurassic Periods? The power of such a beast would be enough to reshape the world as we knew it. A titan emerging for the first time in centuries, ready to lay waste to the world above, summoned forth by Conrad and his hole to China.

Or are these hands just what I can see on the surface, with no deeper meaning? Are they sand worms, popping out to nab a bite before wriggling down just far enough to cover themselves again? Are they staying buried because they're fragile? Because the seagulls and the pelicans which normally scour the beach could have gobbled them up? It seems unlikely, given the acts of violence which I've witnessed today. Fragile doesn't seem like quite the right word.

But the theory isn't impossible.

No, not impossible.

Nothing is impossible at this point.

This morning I would have told you that death was impossible. I was an invincible college student and my friends and I would live forever. We could drink what we wanted. We could do what we wanted. The world was our oyster, or whatever the hell that saying is.

Now I know that's not true. Now I know my place in the universe.

I'm not a coward, but I'm scared; faced with the brutal reality of nature and knowing that I don't matter for a single shit in all of nature's plans. Neither did Conrad. Or Jeanette. Or freaking Kylie. We could be king kahuna, top of our class at school and captain of the football team, or we could be finger food for these monstrosities hidden in the sand. It doesn't matter to the universe one single bit.

I reach the Jeep without realizing it and actually knock my head into the front bumper.

I almost cry as I look up at my sanctuary.

The Jeep is a four-door, black, hardtop which we rented 40 miles closer to civilization. Its tires are old and balding, and it made a concerning rattling noise as we drove it, but in that instant, the car was the most glorious vehicle I'd ever set eyes on.

I twist the towel around and worm my way around to the driver's side door. The mounds in the sand follow me. Even all the way out here, at the car, with me so close to escape, the fingers haven't given up their hope of another meal.

They're patient, as if they know what's going to happen next. An audience in a theater who has been promised a big twist.

I reach the door and stand up, tall, on my towel. The handle is hot as I grasp it. It burns my palm slightly, but I don't care. I grimace against the heat and I pull the handle once.

Twice.

Three times.

The door does not budge.

The Jeep is locked.

I pat my swim trunks, checking the pockets for the key.

I check once. Twice. Three times.

But I understand that I won't find the key.

Conrad had the key.

I turn and look back towards the beach and I see the hole where Conrad was pulled under getting filled by the rising tide. The ocean is washing away any trace of Conrad's activities, just like the fingers had erased his body. Conrad was zero sum in this world. Nothing added. Nothing lost.

By tomorrow morning he would be nothing more than a smooth expanse of beach, and the fingers from the sand would be hungry all over again. Hell, they're still hungry now.

My heart sinks just as I feel something scrape against the side of my foot.

A finger has emerged from the sand, as if sensing my hopelessness. Blood trickles from a cut in the side of my foot, where the finger just dragged its chipped, jagged nail, and I leap up. My feet land on the step bar on the side of the Jeep.

Immediately, almost as if they had planned it, the mounds of sand begin to roll beneath the towel I have abandoned. They bump, nudge, and shift the towel farther and farther away from me until it disappears into the reeds and the sand dunes which we had just travelled through.

I can't watch its progress any farther than that, though, because my hands are on fire.

I'm holding the top of the Jeep, and for a split second I'm not realizing how hot it is. Like when you touch the top of an electric stove on accident, my reaction isn't immediate, but it is violent.

Both of my hands leap into the air, suddenly, and I almost fall backwards before catching myself on the front door's handle. I'm now squatting like an Olympian about to take off in the backstroke, but I can't hold this position for long because the handle burns also.

I'm crying now. Openly bawling like a baby, and below me the sand mounds are swarming around my tears. Are they able to taste me through the tears dripping onto the sand? Do I taste good?

I shimmy to my right. The back driver's side door is locked too. Of course it is. All of the doors are going to be locked. But I need to check them anyhow.

My feet feel fine; the step bar is made of a cool-ish plastic material, but I have to keep moving my hands around constantly to trick them into thinking they aren't being melted from my bones. But they are. I can see that whenever I let go of a door handle. They're red and blisters are already forming around my fingers.

My hands look like the hands from the sand do, and I try not to think too much about what that means. I shuffle my way back to the driver's door.

It's still locked.

I gaze, terrified at the hood of the Jeep and I lift my left leg up. I try to sling the leg onto the hood of the car, to give myself a chance to climb to the other side. Searing pain races up my knee and my calf and my leg kicks backwards, involuntarily, refusing to obey my mind's commands. I shift my handholds.

I imagine crawling across the hood, the skin on my chest sticking to the black metal, peeling away like Elmer's glue being peeled off of a kindergartener. I imagine all of the suffering I would have to endure in order to just jiggle another locked door handle.

I don't want to. I switch my handholds again.

I can't. I switch my handholds again.

I turn to look at the sand mounds collected beneath me. They're uncountable at this point. I shift my hands again, and now there's blood from my skin splitting open.

Maybe Conrad was the lucky one in all of this; dying before he knew what was happening. Maybe the quick, painful death was actually better than the slow, tortured decline of a thousand bad touches.

I imagine what it will be like, clinging to this Jeep for the next few days, waiting to see if somebody happens to come across me out here in the middle of nowhere. I imagine starving. I imagine my hands burning over and over again for hours and hours on end.

I can't stand to hold onto the door's handle any longer.

I let go and my weight carries me away from the Jeep. I see my flesh, ruined and seared beyond recognition as I spin and fall towards the mounds.

Whatever waits for me in the sand, I'll meet them soon.

I'm not a coward.

STORY NOTES:

I still have no clue what the hell drove me to write this story.

More times than not, I approach stories as a pseudo-plotter. I'll have a general outline of where I want the story to go, what sort of kills or ending I want to hit, and then the story might mold or shape itself a little bit differently when I'm actually sitting down and typing it out.

Not the case here.

I started writing this as an entry for Dark Lit Press' Slice of Paradise Anthology (which is amazing. Go read that if you haven't). I wrote the first thousand words without any clue where the story would be going, just that I wanted to write a character who I HATED for once, with no redeeming qualities, who I could kill without remorse. And making it first person? Super weird. I was forcing myself way out of my comfort zone.

For the most part I write characters who I like because I want them to survive. Some do, some don't, but during the journey I prefer living in the headspace of characters who I don't despise while I'm working with them. So this was going to be a departure from my usual comfort zone.

Anyhow, I wrote those first thousand words without any really clear idea of what else would happen in this story. Just the characters. I got this idea in my head that maybe somebody had been buried under the sand and all we could see of them was their fingers still waggling about in the sun and a straw for them to breathe through. Then the jerks who were the main characters would be screwing with the person under the sand.

But then I kept typing and those fingers...killed...someone? I didn't understand it, but it came out. And once it was on the page I couldn't stop.

I still don't fully understand the Lovecraftian monstrosity that lurks beneath the sands of Bad Touch Beach myself. I don't know if I want to. But I think whatever weird subliminal part of me kept pushing this story to be weirder and weirder came up with a fun, ridiculous, splatterpunk idea that's too strange to sell to an anthology, but which is a perfect 'WTF' engine for this collection.

A Once Sensible Girl Loses Her Head

Kat had avoided Old Dutch Bridge for an entire year. It felt strange to be walking up to it now, alone, in the dark of night, but she didn't have much of a choice.

The asphalt under foot was cracked and worn, and Kat's crimson red Converses tread a straight, but apprehensive line towards the sign beside the bridge's entrance. Tomorrow, the town was going to hold a memorial service for Michael Todd. Kat would attend, like she was expected to, but the whole charade of the service felt stupid to Kat. They were holding it on the wrong day, for starters. Michael hadn't died on October 31st. He had died on the 30th. They had just *discovered* his death on Halloween. But, as always, leave it to Tarry to twist the facts into something more entertaining. In small towns like Tarry, facts are always malleable enough to fit their dramatic narratives.

"He died on Halloween," the school children would whisper in hushed tones tomorrow as they rushed from house to house and gathered their candy.

"I heard his ghost haunts Old Dutch Road now," kids would whisper to one another at sleepovers, during the forbidden hours that followed "lights out."

"Maybe he'll come back to get his revenge on Kat for *killing him*," the adults on their porches would suggest, and then they would laugh and pass out their tricks and their treats, and the nights would devolve into the usual acts of youthful vandalism and debauchery which typically punctuated All Hallows Eve.

Kat could practically hear the conversations taking place as she walked, alone, through the cool autumn night. She knew what they would be saying about her because everything about Tarry was so painfully predictable.

She was frustrated and aware of the various ways that the town rumor cycle had spun her story out of control. She hadn't killed the kid. Far from it. But all of the town's stories, no matter which direction their narrative threads seemed to pull initially, circled back to the accident being her fault; as if she had been the one who convinced Michael to drive his motorcycle drunk that night; as if she had been the one who revved the engine and aimed it at the heavy steel sign which removed his head from his shoulders.

It was never the fault of the cop who had let him off with a warning the first time he caught him drunk driving. It was never the fault of the gas station clerk who'd sold him a 40 when he was so clearly underage. It was always Kat, and only Kat, who was villainized in the town's retelling of that night.

A light fog curled around Kat's ankles and she shivered, pulling her hoodie tighter around her chest, over her shoulders.

Her counselor had spent the last year helping her to steel herself against the wounds which resulted from the town's gossip and rumors. Yet still, when everybody in town united behind the same belief, her mental barricades started to falter. If everybody bought into a lie, then the truth died, neglected, in a ditch somewhere.

She supposed that's why she was out here tonight. Not because she wanted to pay her respects to the dead. Not because she wanted to make amends with the past. Instead, Kat was out, alone, well past dark, because this what the town expected from her. She had to play her part in their story. She had to play the apologist. Because she was the one who had rejected Michael, and because that rejection was, in the minds of the good people of Tarry, the catalyst for his binge drinking and driving under the influence.

Now she was expected to play the martyr.

If she didn't come out here tonight, then the whole town would all start telling stories about how she was some heartless bitch. Didn't she care enough about the boy that *she* killed (fuck that), to at least mark the night of his passing?

But Michael had been unstable. He was prone to overreactions. All she had done was reject someone's advances who she had no interest in. She'd even had a boyfriend, Brom, at the time! Why should she have to shoulder the blame for what came next?

She had let him down as nicely as possible.

Kat huffed, her breath coming out in a thick white cloud, and stopped just below an old street lamp poised above the site of the accident. The bushes had grown back, closing off the wound where Michael's motorcycle had torn through them on its way to the river. Grass and detritus filled the tire ruts in the Earth. Mother nature had healed herself over the scars, the head-shaped dent in the bridge sign remaining as the only evidence of the accident.

Kat sat down on the side of the road, hugging her knees to her chest and pointing her Converses at the small pile of tributes which people -who had never known Michael, but who had wanted to make a show of mourning him anyhow- had piled up at the site of the accident. A jack-o-lantern flickered dimly beside four bouquets of flowers, a crude, white, wooden cross, and a picture of Michael from when he was younger, before that desperate flicker of insanity had first crept into his eyes.

Kat sighed.

She really needed to reframe Michael's life in her mind. He hadn't always been as bad as she liked to remember and sure, he had been a little creepy. Sure he seemingly forgot to shower routinely, and his odor had made her nauseous when he sat beside her in Physics, but he had never been truly creepy to her. Not until that last night.

Some deep rumbling engine approached the far side of the bridge, and Kat heard the boards going ca-chunk, ca-chunk, ca-chunk as an automobile rumbled across it.

Good. Finally. She'd only been here for a half a minute, but in her bones, it felt like half a minute too long. She'd needed somebody to drive by, to see her out here carrying out her due diligence, and then the rumor mill would take care of the rest.

Father Prichard's old station wagon finished crossing the bridge, bathing Kat in its headlights, and Kat saw the old pastor give her a small wave as he passed.

Kat exhaled in relief.

Perfect. The gaggle of religious elders who congregated at the church every morning would be a perfect megaphone for her story. They would gobble up the news that Kat was out by the bridge 'mourning her victim' on the first anniversary of his passing. Mr. Prichard would tell Ms. Tillersby, Ms. Tillersby would tell her daughter Sandy, and then everybody would know all about how she had been sobbing uncontrollably at the thought of her lost lover.

She stood, dusted off her jeans, and rolled her perfectly dry eyes- even though that's not the way the story would be told in the morning..

This place was stupid. This ritual was stupid. It was just a cross on the side of the road. Just a dent in a road sign. Nothing more to her. Nothing less. But small town living came with certain strings attached.

Kat spun on her heels and tried to return to her normal life. A Frankenstein and Wolfman movie marathon awaited her back home, the perfect precursor for a good Halloween. Alone. Without Brom around to scoff at the special effects, or belittle her enjoyment. No, with her good deed out of the way, and the glare of the silver screen awaiting her, Kat would spend the night content, putting Michael Todd, his rotting bones, and all of Tarry's bullshit out of sight and out of mind. For a few hours at least.

But as she stepped away, again, Kat heard the sounds of an engine approaching the back side of the bridge.

Kat stepped off the shoulder of the road and stuck her thumb out in the standard hitchhikers pose. It was an awful long walk back to her house from here. Michael couldn't have picked a much more remote place to die without leaving the town's limits.

But as Kat walked, her thumb extended, waiting for the telltale Ca-chunk of a vehicle crossing the bridge, the hairs on the back of her neck slowly stood on end. Because even though the engine behind her was growing louder, the bridge's ancient wooden boards failed to chime in with their half of the song.

Confused, Kat spun back around to face the bridge.

There, just past the wounded sign for Old Dutch Bridge, a motorcycle rumbled, stalled just on the other side of the street light from Kat. The bike's rider was a tall shadow looming over the motorcycle's heavy frame. Though his face was obscured, Kat immediately recognized the rider's posture. She recognized the bike itself. She recognized the strange scent on the air, like body odor semi-masked by too much aerosol cologne.

He was wearing the same awkwardly baggy leather jacket as he had worn the last time Kat saw him. The kind that was supposed to make him look cool, but instead just seemed to accentuate his social incompetence. The rider's face was obscured by the dark of the night, and no matter how hard Kat squinted her eyes, she couldn't make out Michael's face.

So instead, her mind latched onto a more logical answer.

"B-B-Brom?" she asked even though deep in her gut, she knew it wasn't her ex. Brom's shoulders were broader than this person's. Brom was shorter. But Brom was the only person who had known in advance that she was coming out here tonight.

But the other option- that this was somehow Michael Todd straddling his motorcycle in front of her- was too impossible to be considered.

"Listen, Brom. Just because we broke up doesn't mean you can act like an asshole. This shit isn't funny." Then, after a pause. "I thought it was mutual! Would you just…would you just leave me the hell alone?"

The motorcycle rolled forward, slowly, and somehow the darkness seemed to move with it, keeping Brom's head in the shadows.

Kat picked up the Jack-O-Lantern from the dirt near her feet. She reared back and, surprising herself with both her strength and her accuracy, she chucked the pumpkin out of the lamplight, towards the figure in the shadows.

The Jack-O-Lantern lost its top as it spun through the air, but its candle stayed lit just long enough to illuminate the bloody mess of a neck which was all that remained between the motorcyclist's rail-thin shoulder blades.

The light went out when the Jack-O-Lantern crashed to the asphalt.

Kat screamed, the motorcycle roared, and although Kat ran for her life, her Converse's could only move so fast.

--—

The townsfolk of Tally would spend the next three weeks searching for Kat, giving the appearance of a good-faith effort before they gave up the ghost. But it had only taken 24 hours for Father Prichard to tell Ms. Tillersby all about how he had seen the poor girl the night before, just absolutely heartbroken and mourning at the end of the bridge. Ms. Tillersby would then tell her daughter, Sandy, all about how the Father had described Kat, overcome with tears and hardly able to stand up straight due to her agony and heartbreak. Then Sandy would tell the whole school about how Kat had been secretly having an affair with Michael Todd before his accident. Father Prichard had seen it. She would tell them all about how, when that all finally came to light, *that* was why Kat had broken up with Brom. The whole story would be the right mix of plausible and dramatic for the town to buy into it. Brom's denial would only make the gossip even more juicy. Fuel for the fire of Tarry's rumor mill.

By the time the Trick-or-Treaters were out and about that evening, conducting their business as usual, Tally's story would have morphed to embrace these new 'facts.' Their story about the apologetic villain would be forgotten, literally, overnight, and now Kat would just be known as the girl who had always been so dangerously close to losing her mind; a girl who, ever since the death of her secret lover, was so tragically vulnerable that she could just decide to run away from her life at the drop of a hat.

The townsfolk still made a show of looking for her. Because that's what they were *expected* to do. But they did so with their minds on other things. Other rumors. Other gossip.

And why look too hard for a body when you already knew what had happened? Shame could drive a person to do terrible things, they all agreed.

On Wednesday, Ms. Tillersby walked straight
past a flock of vultures which were picking at
oversized roadkill in the ditch beside Sleepy Hollow
Trail. She barely glanced at the carnage. Flies and
blood were grotesque, and they made her feel
squeamish, so she didn't linger for long. She quickly
averted her eyes, like any good Tally citizen did when
reality proved itself to be distasteful.

Nobody would walk the trail after her. At least,
not before the ditch was covered with a fresh blanket
of fallen leaves.

By the end of three weeks, people stopped
pretending to look all together. Finding the body at
that point would have ruined the narrative they'd
settled on: the cautionary tale of an ungrateful young
lady who had thrown her life away, holding her own
pride in higher regard than the interests of a boy as
nice as Michael Todd; of a girl who had driven him to
his tragic death; and who had finally been so
overcome with remorse that she fled town forever.
The once respectable girl had lost her head and this
was, apparently, the price.

It was just such a shame that she hadn't been nicer to start with. Any *respectable* girl would have been.

The adults never paid any mind to the stories that the town's youths told every Halloween from then on. Stories about the strange motorcyclist who rode around the edge of town. A headless rider carving a path along Tarry's back roads, a severed head tucked under his arm which looked remarkably similar to Katherine Holloway. A head with its lips curled back in a perpetual scream, the eyes leaking tears which stained their cheeks a thick, sticky red.

Those silly ghost stories didn't matter to the residents of Tarry, New York.

They only cared about *real* stories.

STORY NOTES:

Hey look! It's another short story that I wrote for a specific call.

This time I got inspired by the call for James Aquilone's Classic Monsters Unleashed anthology. The idea was to take a classic monster story (in this case, the Headless Horseman) and to update it for the modern era. Not just in the "make the horse a motorcycle" sense, but to get the message it sends up to code as well.

So with the Legend of Sleepy Hollow, I kind of hate Ichabod Crane. He's a whiny, jealous, sore loser pining for the hand of...his student? What the hell? No. Stop. This isn't to say that Brom is the person Katrina should have ended up with. He's a bully and the modern equivalent of the cruel jock in a bad teen sitcom. But there had to be more options for Kitrina in that village besides JUST these two...right?

Anyhow. My story.

I wanted this to be Katrina's story. I wanted to see this macho, bravado, bullshit contest through her

eyes, and I also wanted to grapple with the
consequences of the original Sleepy Hollow story.
Because it wouldn't all just end with Crane's death,
would it? The village would go out, trying to discover
what happened to the one school teacher in town
when he didn't show up for work again. Who would
get blamed? The mythical being in the woods? Maybe.
But more likely society would blame the woman,
wouldn't they? In the story, Katrina's rejection of
Crane is a pretty public event. So when he went off
and disappeared immediately after that, anybody who
cared would turn their accusatory glances towards
Kitrina. She HAD been a flirt. She HAD led Ichabod
on. And now it had killed him. Or at least driven him
away.

What would that do to her?

Well. Here's my best shot at answering.

And what's more, that's the end of the
collection! Thanks so much for reading these with me.
I'm going to conclude with the usual end-pages, with
plugs for my novels included, but before we devolve
into that, I just want to give a big, wholehearted thank
you for giving these stories a chance. We got kind of

weird there, didn't we? Maybe a little dark in parts? I hope you found something that connected with you in these pages. Whether it was Lewellyn fleeing from the Mothman or Kendall finally snapping, my fingers are crossed that something put a sick, twisted smile on your face, if just for a moment. I hope you'll join me again for more stories later.

A Note From The Author:

Thanks so much for reading IRRATIONAL FEARS. I hope at least one story in this collection made you smile or gave you the heebie jeebies.

If you feel so inclined, it would mean the world if you could leave a review on Amazon or Goodreads,

Other books by me include:

Through Frozen Veins- Closed Room Supernatural Horror Mystery

Through Withered Roots- Small Town Disappearances Horror

Killer Be Killed- Reverse Camp Slasher Horror

Synapse- Dystopian, Memory Selling Horror

Stay Spooky.

William Sterling.

Made in the USA
Monee, IL
17 September 2022

14116653R00105